Masters of Time

A Science Fiction and Fantasy Time Travel Anthology

By Alesha Escobar, Devorah Fox, H.M. Jones, Samantha LaFantasie, Alice Marks, and Timothy C. Ward

First Print Edition

Published by Creative Alchemy, Inc.

Edited by Charmaine M. Young

Cover Art by Luis E. Escobar

http://www.thecreativealchemy.com

ISBN-13: 978-1514173725

ISBN-10: 1514173727

DEDICATION

To the future, and all who hope to make it better.

CONTENTS

ACKNOWLEDGMENTS

All creative endeavors have an inspiration, and it takes talent, dedication, and heart to bring them to life. I am very grateful for the turn of fate that has brought the brilliant Masters of Time authors together, its amazing editor, Ms. Young, and of course, the artistic genius of Luis Escobar.

--Alesha Escobar

LOGAN 6

The ballerina's nostrils flared as she paused to wipe away the tears streaming down her cheek. She wasn't a nurse, but she was the closest thing he had to one. Logan wanted to tell her to stop crying, that he wasn't going to hurt her and only wanted her to patch up his shoulder before he bled to death. But he knew it would only make her cry even more.

"Gah!" He bit his lower lip when the automated medi-gun stabbed him behind his right shoulder, injecting a million nanobots into his wound. He let out a slow gasp, wondering if he seemed squeamish or weak to her.

Why do I care? This isn't the time for that. He glanced over at his tracker. The sleek, gray device, the length of the palm of his hand, stood silent and gave off not a single red blip on its screen. The Core Guardsman in black military fatigues had apparently left the area. It would be safe now to leave this point in time.

"I have fifty dollars in my purse. Take it." The ballerina's voice quivered as she placed the gun on the desk and reached for her sweater. She wiped her hands hastily as if being exposed to his blood would somehow infect her.

Logan rotated his nearly healed shoulder and reached for his soiled shirt. A dark stain marred the back shoulder area where his pursuer had shot him. He threw on his shirt and slipped off the large dark desk, hitting the floor with his heavy feet.

"I told you I don't want to rob you. I'm not going to hurt you."

He heard footsteps and a knock at the door. In a flash, he reached for his laser gun, and the ballerina quietly sobbed. Logan raised his index finger to his lips, gesturing for her to be quiet. He mouthed the words, "Who is it?"

"M-my students," she whispered, just as a few more knocks and the voices of young girls filled the hallway outside. Why Doctor Simmons ever decided it was a great idea to hide an emergency access point behind a dance school's wall was beyond him. Maybe it was a clever thing he didn't understand about humans.

He motioned for her to go across the room to the door. Even when in abject fear, she knew how to move gracefully. Her willowy arm reached for the doorknob, and she halted and turned toward him with a questioning look. He nodded in response.

She turned the knob and cracked the door open just enough to stick her head through while blocking the rest of the opening with her lean body. "Okay, give me five minutes, girls. I'll be ready."

A few whiny voices protested. It sounded like one of them asked her if she had been crying. Logan's stomach clenched, and he held his breath. The ballerina delivered a fake chuckle and said she had a cold.

Yeah, in damn July...he thought to himself.

Hmph. He wished Riley would've been here to hear that thought. The lab assistant would've been amused that the curse words he occasionally let slip actually stuck with Logan. The ballerina shut the door and slowly approached him. Her gaze seemed to go past him, as if she were looking for something. He nodded toward her.

"I'll be out of your hair—or bun—soon." He slipped his laser gun into his holster and pocketed the tracker. He walked over to the only wall in the room lined with mirror panels.

He gazed at his reflection, noting the wear and tear he had accrued on this trip. A black eye, swollen nose, a bulging knot on the head, and of course the laser gun shot that nearly bled him out. And he hadn't a shred of useful information on the whereabouts of the man called Adam. Doctor Simmons would have a fit. Hell, with any luck, Simmons's head would explode.

Logan scratched the stubble on his chin and turned his left wrist. The indicator on his access watch lit up, and a faint light pulsed from behind the mirror panel farthest to the right. He rushed over to the panel and carefully removed it, the sense of urgency growing in him as the little ballerinas outside began clamoring at the door again.

"What are you doing?" the woman asked. A strong, clear voice now replaced the shrill one she had used earlier, and it made Logan shift his position and watch her from the corner of his eye.

"I'm going home."

He stood and waited for the sequence numbers on the screen installed in the wall to match those on his access watch. When the numbers read the same, he punched his code into the buttons beneath the screen. The pulses from the interface on the wall became a low hum, and though no windows were open, a strong breeze swept through the room. To his surprise, the woman didn't cry or run in the opposite direction. She approached, startled, but oddly had a look of recognition in her eyes.

"Where are you from?" Her voice no longer quivered. Wisps of dark hair framing her face blew in several directions.

Logan watched a portal of light form in front of him. He turned to face her. "Another time."

Her eyes narrowed. "You're one of *them*, aren't you? You want to kill Adam."

Not quite the goodbye he was expecting. "Your leader is a murderer...a usurper."

"*Liar.*" She rushed over to her desk.

"Hey—don't call the Core Guard, lady. I'm leaving."

Her hazel eyes flashed with anger as she brandished her own laser gun. Oh. So she *wasn't* calling the Core Guard. He should've known better than to have been distracted by her emotional display.

"My *name* is Anika!"

She aimed at him. His adrenaline kicked in and his heart pounded in his chest as he dove into the portal of light. Far from being warm and safe, the portal thrashed him around like a rag doll—one that had been sucked into a large vacuum. Luckily, the unpleasant sensation and blinding light only lasted seconds. He lost his bearings and his legs folded beneath him.

The light vanished and the whirlwind quieted. He felt the familiar cold floor of the Time Access Chamber, or TAC for short, pressing against his throbbing face. He forced himself to his feet, and before he could even reach the door and use his access watch to open it, Doctor Simmons came in with his annoying aerial recorder. "Aero," a mechanical sphere, hummed and flew in a tight circle around Logan before scanning him.

"Aero," Simmons said in his gravelly voice, "begin recording."

Ping! Aero ended its scanning and a green light flickered in its circular center. Logan never liked Aero. It always reminded him that he was being watched, and the irony wasn't lost on him that the machine resembled a huge eye.

"Doctor Simmons…" Logan swallowed and forced the knotting in his stomach to quell. His eyesight blurred, but he knew Simmons wouldn't want to hear about that. "The Free Army is closing in, and its advocates are winning more citizens over to our side."

"I hear a *but* coming…" he prodded the knot on Logan's head with his silver pen, which made him suck in a sharp breath.

"The Core Guard interrupted what should've been a meeting with my contact. If I can find Jeremy again, we'll know where Adam is."

The scientist ran a hand through his curly brown hair. "Jeremy never showed up? He may have just taken the money and ran."

"Or, he was scared. I can try again."

"We'll see."

Aero zipped dangerously close to Logan's head. He had to resist the urge to swat it like a fly. "Doctor, if we're done…I'd like pain medication and rest."

Simmons waved his hand dismissively. "Next time try not to get into a direct fight with the guardsmen if you can help it. I can't afford to lose you."

Logan had seen old films where people would say that to one another with conviction. Simmons said it in a way a parent would tell his kid not to get a dent in the car because it was expensive merchandise. In fact, he *was* the merchandise. He was an enhanced clone, a class all its own. Close enough to human for most of them to tolerate his existence, yet not human enough to be treated like one.

"Thank you, Doctor." Logan's head throbbed again.

"And, before I end this recording…what year is it right now?"

"2062 AD."

"And the year at the point of exit, right before you returned to us."

Logan squinted. "2081 AD."

Simmons's eyebrows shot up. "Good. We got you in a year earlier this time. We'll see if we can push for 2080. The quicker we can get to Adam, the sooner we can prevent the catastrophe—"

A rapping at the door interrupted them, and a young man with ketchup stains on his lab coat and hair as curly as the doctor's slipped inside the TAC. "Uh…Doctor Simmons,"

"What is it, Riley?" Simmons snapped.

"My mom's on the phone for you."

"Aero, end recording." The machine made another pinging noise, and the green light in the center faded to black. It flew over and hovered above the doctor. "Riley, administer 40 mg of propofol to Logan 6. It ought to take care of the pain and help it sleep. What does my sister want?"

Riley shrugged his shoulders. He adjusted his lab coat to hide the ketchup stains. "Something about her birthday next week."

Simmons shook his head, probably regretting ever bringing his nephew on as an assistant. He turned and left the chamber. Aero followed swiftly behind.

"Logan…" Riley's eyes widened. "You look like shit. What happened to you, man?"

Logan's knees buckled, and Riley rushed to support him—which wasn't easy since the kid was thinner than a pole. One thing Logan did like about being a modified clone was his strength, speed, and well-built physique. But that didn't mean much when you've had your ass beaten and have been shot in the shoulder with a Raven-220 laser gun.

"Can I get my meds?" Logan winced when Riley tried to hold him and walk in step at the same time. He added a fractured rib to his list of injuries.

"Sure, buddy."

Riley walked him out to the main corridor and down a few doors to the infirmary. Logan slunk onto the cot in the corner and let the young man administer the sedative. At first his veins were on fire, but the warm numbness that spread throughout had finally dulled the pain.

"Riley." Logan closed his eyes. "Why do we have an emergency access point in the old town district—on 9th and Lincoln?"

"Did that propofol go to your head already? Logie, we don't have an access point there."

"*Don't* call me Logie."

Riley chuckled. "Goodnight. I'll see you in the morning."

***

Logan awoke feeling groggy. His belly ached with hunger. Despite the infirmary cot feeling like a wooden plank, he wanted to lie there and savor the last few wisps of dreams that visited him. Sometimes he'd dream of hunting for Adam the Usurper twenty years in the future, or of Doctor Simmons sending Aero to burrow into his head and steal his most secret thoughts and desires. But at the first light of dawn, he had held the pleasant image of Anika the Ballerina. In his dream, she'd smile instead of weep at him. Her hair would fall in loose, dark waves, crowning her face and grazing her toned, bronze shoulders. She'd dance gracefully for him.

"Hey, buddy…wake up!" Riley came in cradling a change of clothes and clean towels.

Logan frowned and remembered that he hadn't changed out of the bloodstained clothing from last night. He sat up and accepted the pile from the young man. He muttered a thanks.

"Don't mention it. Connelly's here today to evaluate you. He says to be in room 13 in an hour."

"I'll be there."

Riley left, and Logan let out a frustrated sigh. He liked Ward Connelly, but he didn't want to go through an evaluation today. He wanted to find out why his tracker led him to an emergency time access point where there shouldn't have been one. He wanted to know why Anika didn't have a break down over him saying he was from another time. And most of all, he wanted to know why today was different from any other day he's had.

He took a quick shower and changed clothes, all the while pondering how he could wake up wanting something that *he* wanted, not what he anticipated Simmons or the General wanted. He knew his makers had strategically diminished some of his capacities— mainly his emotions—but it seemed the harder they tried to eradicate these faculties, the more they ferociously clung to him.

Did this mean he was more than a mere clone? Simmons had never referred to Logan in a personal manner. As far as the doctor was concerned, Logan was a high-functioning *it* that could speak, spy, fight, report events, and if need be, die. Although no one ever spoke to him about it, he had become convinced that there must have been a Logan 1 and 2, all the way up to 5. So, what happened to them? Did Simmons destroy them because they couldn't complete their task? Or did they die in the streets of future Ithaca City?

These agitating questions swarmed in the back of his mind as he met with Doctor Ward Connelly in room 13. The psychologist had opened some of the blinds to let the sunshine in, and he had a cup of hot coffee waiting for Logan. He took his seat at the L-shaped white table across from Connelly. He wanted all the warmth the morning sun had to give.

"I hear you ran into some trouble, Logan." Connelly covered his cough with his right hand. "Excuse me. It seems the older I get, the more this body of mine wants to break down."

"I'll probably break down before you, Doctor."

"Just...Connelly. There's only one man in this building with a stick up his ass who wants you to call him Doctor all the time."

The comment elicited a smile from Logan. "I...had more dreams last night."

"Oh?" Connelly arched a gray eyebrow. He listened to Logan explain yesterday's assignment, of Simmons's frustration with him, and of course, about meeting Anika. Well, as much as it could be called a meeting after bursting into her dance class demanding that she heal him with a medi-gun because he couldn't reach the injured area by himself. He didn't think making a woman cry garnered a good first impression.

"What is it?" Logan asked in response to Connelly's piercing gaze.

The psychologist stood with the help of his black cane and went over to the open blinds. His leathery, dark hand gestured toward the outside world. "Tell me what you see down there."

He joined the doctor at the window, noting the skyline of Ithaca City, with its lush trees that sprouted in its greener side, and the symmetric buildings, homes, and businesses in the urban sections. But what Connelly wanted him to see was the gate that separated the IthaCorp facility from the mob of protestors below, holding signs and shouting.

"*Get Out of Bed With the Government, IthaCorp!*" one read. Another said to "*Free the Clones.*" The majority of them, however, saved their damnations for Logan and those like him.

"Hmm." Logan snorted, trying to control the strain in his voice. "*Walking-Talking Toe Nail Clipping* is a new one."

"You're angry." Connelly stroked his white beard.

"Do you think I am what they say I am?"

"Only *you* can define who you are. So you didn't start off like the rest of us, but you're made of the same stuff, albeit enhanced. You've got the capacity to reason, and from the sound of your encounter with that young lady, you also know beauty when you see it."

Logan decided not to acknowledge the last part of Connelly's comment. He turned his gaze back toward the crowd outside. IthaCorp security began rolling out an armored vehicle and over a hundred overgrown Aeros, except these had been weaponized.

A collective silence hushed the throng of protestors. They dispersed on their own. And they were smart to do so. Among the many powers given to IthaCorp by the United Americas government, was that of lethal self-defense.

Connelly cleared his throat. "Those people out there were happy to accept clones going to war for them, and for taking dangerous jobs in our colonies, but the moment IthaCorp moved to make you more than their fodder, they no longer saw our destinies intertwined with each other."

Logan turned away and headed for the L-shaped table. He grabbed his cup of coffee and took a sip. Connelly joined him, reaching into his right pocket and tossing a square, metallic object onto the table. No larger than an ice cube, he scooped it up and placed it into his own pocket. A smile flickered across his lips.

"What's this one about?"

Connelly hid another hoarse cough beneath a chuckle. "It has adventure, peril, and some dancing."

"Thanks."

The doctor approached and stuck his hand in his briefcase sitting across from Logan. He took out his digital notepad, checking off a list for his report. "Don't mention it. My wife would actually see it as you doing us a favor. She's been nagging me about getting rid of those old movies for fifteen years now."

"Can I ask you something?"

"Of course."

"What happened to the other Logans?"

Connelly's nostrils flared, and he eyed Logan up and down, sizing him up. "That's a delicate question."

The door opened from the far right. The General stepped into the room, trailed by Doctor Simmons. The stocky General looked like he hadn't worn his faded gray combat suit and tactical vest in years. He probably only put it on for some of the news cameras outside catching the protests.

"I thought *you* were the one who's supposed to be asking questions, Connelly." The General gave him a cursory nod.

"I'll do my job, General Wilde, and you'll do yours." Connelly coughed into his elbow.

The General sneered. "The three of us need to talk. Now."

Doctor Simmons cleared his throat. "Logan, why don't you go down to the TAC. We'll be sending you off soon."

He gave Simmons a blank expression, all the while shocked at hearing he would be sent back through time so soon. They usually gave him three days to recover. "Sure, Doctor."

He stepped outside and closed the door behind him. He pressed his left ear into the door, straining to hear the conversation among the three men. He caught General Wilde's voice first—his was always the loudest and most grating.

"...So I think you've proven it could be done with clones. Now I'm interested in starting human trials again..."

A hacking cough from Connelly followed. "It will kill a regular human."

"We need a *real* person to go into the Time Access Chamber," Simmons's gravelly voice said. "Don't give us that crap about time travel killing people when—"

Connelly cut him off. "You lost your say in the matter when you sabotaged Logan 5."

Logan stepped backward, his hands trembling as he turned away and headed toward the TAC lab. He had suspected as much, but still, it was difficult to hear the truth. However, there were still pieces to the puzzle missing, and he needed to find out what they were—before he ended up like the other Logans.

"Good morning, Logan 6," a dark-haired woman in a lab coat said with a smile. She came from the opposite direction down the hall.

"Good morning, Karen." He gave a curt nod. He didn't slow his pace, he needed to get to the lab.

"I've made some adjustments to your diet. I'll let Doctor Simmons know."

"Thanks." He passed her, motioning toward the TAC lab to let her know he couldn't stop to discuss meals.

He lowered his head when another doctor, an IthaCorp security guard, and a lab technician passed him in the hallway as well. He went into the TAC lab, eyeing not the door to the time travel chamber, but the man sitting at the control panel—Riley.

Logan cringed at the abrasive music blaring from Riley's headphones. It was a wonder the guy could still hear. He tapped him on the shoulder, and the young man swiveled in a startled movement, removing his headphones.

"Oh, hey…hey." He turned the ugly music off, thank goodness. "For a second, I thought you were my uncle."

Logan grinned. "Lucky for you, I'm not. He'd let you have it for forgetting to put in the order."

Riley ran a hand through his dark brown curls. "What order?"

"The flowers. For your mother's birthday." Logan hated lying to him, but he wanted the kid to have no part in what he was about to do.

"I don't remember…"

"That's why you guys invented me. Perfect memory. I thought I'd remind you, since it looked like you weren't paying attention when he told you. You know how Doctor Simmons is when he opens his mouth."

Riley chuckled. "Tell me about it. Thanks for the heads up. Where do I put in the order?"

"Le Fleur. You need to call in now, if you want it done in time." When Logan saw the young man reach for the call button, he added, "Why don't you call from Karen's office?"

Riley's bony index finger hovered above the red button. He gave Logan a crooked smile. "It's that obvious, huh?"

"I just passed her in the hallway, and she asked about you. Pretend Simmons sent you to talk to her about my new diet. You can call the flower shop from there and talk with her."

"Karen asked about me?" He was already on his feet and shedding his wrinkled lab coat.

"Well, are you going to stand here all day? Your uncle's going to be out of his meeting with the General."

"Okay. I'll be right back."

Riley nearly stumbled through the doorway. Logan waited a few seconds before locking the door. He rummaged through the other man's lab coat hanging on the chair. His fingers tightened when he grabbed the keycard. He slipped it into a slot and entered a code: 87543. He had seen Simmons do it before when updating records uploaded from Aero or when performing a manual entry.

The large screen above the control panel turned from black to white, and Doctors Simmons and Connelly stood side-by-side, facing the camera. Connelly let out a cough and spoke.

"When we started this, we had agreed to never do the past. We would observe the future, learn from it, and perhaps…avoid any cataclysms, if possible. It's been two months since Logan 1 has been sent twenty years into the future. In that regard, our project can be considered a success—time travel, with an enhanced clone, is possible. However, the obvious disappearance of Logan is worrisome. Either something prevented him from returning through the TAC, or he is deceased."

Simmons cleared his throat. "We've prepared Logan 2 and will be sending him in one hour. His instructions are to find Logan 1, or at least find out what happened to him."

The screen went to black and lit up again. This time, Simmons faced the screen alone.

"Doctor Connelly is in the infirmary. It seems his use of the TAC last year could prove fatal. We'll continue monitoring his health."

Logan's stomach tightened and he balled his fists. "Son of a…"

So, that was the source of Connelly's mysterious illness. The old man had actually traveled through time. However, it took a toll on his body, unlike the Logans. He had to rewind the recording because he had missed what Simmons had said.

The recording of Simmons continued. "…and General, sir, I know you see the return of Logan 2 as a success, but we should treat his report about the future with the urgency it deserves. Logan 2 *must* return and terminate Logan 1. If the United Americas government ever found out about this…" He gulped, then instructed Aero to end the recording.

Logan ran through the subsequent recordings: Logan 2 never returned from his assassination mission. An updated Logan 3, with more enhancements and designed to be more obedient, returned, but had failed. Simmons had him "terminated" as a precaution. An appended recording, narrated by the voice of a distraught Doctor Connelly, showed Logan 2 finally returning through the TAC—but then attacking Simmons and inadvertently killing a female lab assistant who had been there. IthaCorp security rushed in and sliced up Logan 2 with their laser guns. Simmons held the lifeless woman in his arms, sobbing over her.

Logan drew in a deep breath, blood pounding in his ears, and played the last recording. Logan 4, who was as compliant as Logan 3 had been, returned from the TAC with a gaping, bloody wound in his side. It looked like the Core Guards from the future had done him in good. He didn't make it, either.

In the last half of the video, Connelly faced the screen, pausing to cough up blood into a wad of tissue. He claimed the first Logan now went by the name of Adam, and had forged an impressive new society, where clones and humans could live together—but it was being held back by the Free Army and their sympathizers, and those who had financial and military interests in keeping clones as a sub-class. In a pained voice, he said Simmons would be absent from the lab while Logan 6 was being prepared; the scientist, in his grief, had sabotaged Logan 5 and gotten the clone killed. Logan 6 would be the last, and if he didn't succeed, they'd have to dismantle the entire program and admit to the government's Scientific Oversight Committee what IthaCorp had done.

The screen faded to black.

Logan didn't need a hint as to what his fate would be if the program were dismantled. With sweaty palms, he slipped the keycard back into Riley's lab coat pocket, reeling from the fact that all this time, he had been asked to go into the future and murder a clone brother—himself, in a sense—one whose only crime was being more than what some men wanted him to be.

It made him angry, as angry as Logan 2 who had returned from the future with bulging eyes and veins popping in his neck. Did he learn the truth, too? Was that why he came back here in a rage?

A pounding at the lab door ripped him from his thoughts and questions. He heard Simmons's gravelly voice, an octave higher than usual, demanding that Logan unlock the lab entrance or else IthaCorp security would be called. When Logan heard the beeping of an override code being entered into the digital lock panel on the other side of the door, he bolted toward the TAC and turned it on.

He synced his access watch with the familiar light portal. A soft breeze caressed his cheek, as if welcoming him. Just as the breeze grew into a whirlwind, he looked back at the chamber's window to see Simmons rush in with five IthaCorp security guards. A stunned Doctor Connelly joined them, but he gave Logan a subtle nod, as if saying he understood what was happening.

The speaker came on, and a seething Doctor Simmons spoke. "You piece of *shit* clone. Get back here, now!"

He kept his eyes on the window, eyeing the two doctors and the guards with apprehension. He backed into the portal, knowing that they wouldn't risk coming inside the chamber while the access point was open. Not unless they all wanted to die.

"I'm sorry, Doctor Simmons. I'm sorry about what Logan 2 did."

Wisps of light, bursting with energy, slid along Logan's skin and began pulling him toward the greater part of the access point. He met Simmons's gaze and saw the scientist's expression soften. He almost looked like a statue.

He suddenly leaned forward, face screwing up in rage. "Don't ever talk to me about that. You don't get to talk to me about her. Now, shut down the TAC and come out."

Logan shook his head. He no longer hated Simmons. He finally understood why he acted the way he did toward him, though it was no fault of his. Logan 2 was to blame. "I'm sorry."

Logan stretched out his arms and threw himself backward, into the light.

***

The old warehouse on 24th street still smelled like damp wood and rat droppings. Logan took a few seconds to rub his sore knees and recover from the head-spinning that overtook him from traveling through the TAC. When he was certain that he wasn't going to vomit or swoon, he walked over to the south side of the abandoned warehouse.

He used the sunlight beaming from holes in the roof to guide him. He felt his way along the wall until he located the false wooden panel where he had stored clothes and supplies from an earlier trip. He quickly exchanged his simple lab clothes for an authentic Core Guard uniform. He had been saving it for an emergency, or for when he was able to actually catch up with Logan 1, who was apparently Adam. He still wanted to catch up with him, but this time, it wasn't in order to kill him. He wasn't what he wanted to do next, to be honest. But he knew he needed to see Adam for himself, to speak with him face-to-face.

Logan walked briskly down the alley toward the main street, making a sharp right turn. He tensed when he saw a large crowd of people gathered, with several units of Core Guards strung throughout. They lined the sidewalks but kept the street clear. When the crowd began cheering at a motorcade of sleek black cars with the Ithaca United Core symbol, he realized that he had walked in on a procession.

He spotted at least three high-ranking Core members who served under Adam. They waved at the crowd and saluted the Core Guards as they passed. One of the members had an amplified speaker in his car, and he began rattling off phrases such as: "The Free Army isn't for freedom, but slavery." "The United Core will unite *all* people, whether natural-born or clone." "We have no future, unless we learn from the mistakes of our past." They even had a preacher in the motorcade, waving a worn, leather-bound Bible.

Hmph. Looked like Adam was smart. He knew who to surround himself with and how to speak to people. Did he really believe in all this? Or was this some type of battle tactic in order to win the greater war? This whole time he had been conditioned to believe that the Free Army were the ones standing for liberty and a safe future, but they were really the creation of military and corporate interests, and their foot soldiers the prejudiced and privileged who would send clones like Adam and Logan to war, work the coal mines or oil rigs, but never to sit next to them in a college classroom or pray next to them in a church.

He gave a curt nod to a few Core Guards as he followed the motorcade. His only lead to Adam would have to be one of the men or women in those sleek black cars. Just when the procession of cars turned at Lincoln to go past 23rd Street, a pair of bright hazel eyes, wide nose, and pouty lips emerged in the sea of faces. Logan's breath caught in his throat.

Anika.

The dancer. The woman who had looked at him and knew what he was and where he had come from. What if *she* knew where Adam was? Despite his brain telling him to just follow the motorcade with the politicians and dignitaries, something deep within his gut pulled him toward Anika.

He approached her, almost entranced, and was within reach of her when she turned and caught a glimpse of him. Her jaw dropped, and her eyes widened with recognition. Just as she turned to a neighbor next to her and shouted something to him, the bodies pressing against them in the crowd opened their mouths in elated unison and shouted "United Core, freedom for all!"

Anika turned in the opposite direction and snaked through the crowd toward a *real* Core Guard. Logan lunged after her, grabbing her by the wrist. She spun on her heel and swung her fist at him. She landed a hit next to his right eye. It stunned him. He ignored the throbbing pain and pulled her toward him.

"Where's Adam?" He whispered harshly into her ear.

"You're hurting me."

He loosened his grip. "Sorry."

A flash of pain and a fleeting vision of stars hit him again. Anika had broken through the crowd and was running down Lincoln Street before he realized she had whacked him again.

Logan cursed and pushed his way past a group of teenagers watching the procession. Who the hell was this woman? He never knew a dainty ballerina could land punches like that. At least, none he ever saw in the films Doctor Connelly had given him. He was torn between anger and sheer fascination.

He chased her down the street, pulling out his gun and firing a warning shot when she tried to hail a cab. The few people in the area who weren't at the procession with the entire city assumed she had gotten into trouble. He thanked the stars that his Core Guard uniform came in handy.

In keeping with his disguise, he handcuffed her when he caught up to her. He pulled her along and walked her down the street, turning a corner. He took her another block before slipping into an alley with her. When he spun her around to face him, he waited for her to begin pleading with him. However, she just glared at him defiantly, in silence.

"You're not going to talk now?" He wanted to massage the side of his face where she had hit him, but he resisted the urge.

"Why should I? You're just like the other clones they sent. Don't you think for yourself? Can't you see that they're using you to get to Adam? And when they don't need you anymore, what do you think's going to happen?"

He glanced at a few people walking past the alley. They didn't notice him and Anika. He gazed at her. "I'm supposed to be the last.

They were going to get rid of me too. I'm here because I want to meet Adam."

And he certainly had nowhere else to go. If he even dared go back through the TAC, he'd be sliced up like the other Logan. For better or worse, this time was where he had to stay.

"I don't believe you." Her nostrils flared, in the same way they did when he had barged into her dance class that day.

"If I were here to do their bidding, then you would be dead. Right? I told you, I don't want to hurt you."

"Then un-cuff me."

"No way. I've learned my lesson."

She bit her lower lip. "It's funny you're looking for Adam, because he was right next to me when I spotted you."

Logan's pulse began racing. "That man with the short blond hair, scar on his right cheek, wearing the green jacket, black boots, and a silver ring on his right hand?"

She nodded, unable to hide her amazement at his detailed description. "I told him it was too dangerous to walk around like that. But he told me he wanted to be among the people. He said he didn't want to wait until the Free Army was destroyed—he wanted to be a leader for Ithaca *today*."

"Hmph. I'm starting to like this Adam. Did you know he was born Logan 1?"

Her eyes narrowed. "And which one are you?"

"Logan 6, but I'm *not* trying to kill him like the others were. It...was smart of you to break away, so I wouldn't discover him."

"Just take me to my dance class. Adam will come looking for me."

"Why?"

"Just do it."

***

Logan slid out of the dark vest with the Core Guard insignia, leaving a black undershirt beneath. He muttered a thanks to Anika when she handed him a cup of cold water. He drank it down in a few gulps, then, suddenly, remembered that he couldn't fully trust her.

She must've seen the expression on his face, because she smirked and waved her hand dismissively. "Don't worry, it's plain old water."

"Well, you did punch me twice and tried to shoot me." He ran a hand through his short, dark hair.

She crossed her arms, leaning against the edge of her desk. "What are you going to do when Adam gets here?"

"If he's willing to talk...we'll talk. If he wants to fight, I'll be ready for that, too." He grabbed his Raven-300 silver laser gun and checked its energy level. He shoved it into his pocket.

"I knew you were one of them. You might look different, but I could tell. It's the eyes."

His olive skin tone and dark eyes contrasted with the first Logan's blond hair and green eyes, but they had a similar muscular build and looked like they could be brothers, if not close relatives. Some of the other Logans had hair ranging from dark brown to fiery red; it seemed when they adjusted the mental faculties of each one, they decided to also tinker with physical appearance as well.

Logan motioned toward the glass panel where the time access interface remained hidden. "Who built that? It's not ours."

Her eyebrows shot up. "My father built it. He's one of the first of the Core Guard. You can thank him for teaching me how to fight. He believes in Adam."

"Who is your father?"

"Ward Connelly, Jr."

Logan raised an eyebrow. "I should've seen it. I know your grandfather, Doctor Connelly. Is he in the city?"

She shook her head and frowned. "He died, twenty years ago, when I was just a kid."

Damn. Connelly's illness had destroyed him. So much for General Wilde's human trials. With virtually no allies around, Logan began wondering if he were better off contacting his informant, Jeremy, and hitching a ride out of Ithaca City.

"I'm sorry to hear about Connelly. He was the only man who treated me like a person." He may have been resentful over the doctor never telling him that he had used the TAC, but Connelly had done so many other things for him. His chest tightened with pain.

Anika gave him a grateful nod. "Thank you."

"What about General Wilde and Doctor Simmons?

"Your wonderful friends at IthaCorp made sure General Wilde took all the blame for what happened. They lied and planted evidence. They did whatever it took."

"I'm not surprised. And what about Simmons?"

The door to the classroom swung open. Doctor Simmons stepped in, flanked by four armed men in dark gray fatigues. Anika gazed at him in astonishment, and Logan could hardly conceal his surprise. The doctor he had known twenty years ago was barely recognizable. Wrinkles spread across his forehead and beneath his eyes. His face looked pale, and his once brown, curly hair was now white and sparse, and he wore thick glasses.

"Simmons is still alive and kicking, Logan. I can't tell you how long I've waited for this day. Oh, wait, I've been waiting twenty years for this. Come in, Jeremy."

Jeremy, who was supposed to be Logan's informant, stepped into the room, brandishing a red and gray laser gun. The short, pudgy man wore a lazy grin. "Sorry, Logan, but you couldn't find me on your last trip here because I was meeting with Simmons. Met with him again after you ran from his lab twenty years back. What can I say? I have been, and always will be, on his payroll."

Simmons gave Logan a smug look. "You've become distracted. Jeremy was in the crowd, shadowing you, but you only saw her. You only cared about her." He approached Anika and grabbed her by her arm, the tip of his laser gun pressing into her cheek. She let out a yelp.

"Let her go," Logan growled. The four men trained their weapons on him.

"If Adam hands himself over without a fight," Simmons said, "I'll let her go. I'm not a monster, Logan."

"Liar!" Anika didn't back down when Simmons snarled at her and tried to muffle her with his forearm. She bit him.

"You *little…*" He tried to slap her, but she slipped out of his grasp, dipped low, and delivered a kick to his stomach. She grabbed his gun just as the armed men aimed at her, but they seemed hesitant to shoot, since she now had control of the gun and was shoving its tip right into Simmons's cheek.

"Doesn't feel good, does it?" She tightened her grip on the gun.

"Anika, don't!" Simmons pleaded in a shrill voice. "I knew you as a child, and now you've been *poisoned* by Adam and his nonsense. You can't shoot me. You're not a murderer."

"Quiet." Though she commanded him in a steady voice, her hand trembled.

Jeremy tossed his red and gray over to Logan at his beckoning; he

18

already had his Raven-300 pointed at him. The four men slid their laser guns across the floor toward Anika before holding their hands up in surrender. Just when Logan was about to demand they also give up any backup weapons, two of the henchmen drew laser guns from inside their coat pockets and fired.

Logan dove to the side, but a razor sharp pain in his left leg told him that one of the laser shots had tore through him. He clenched his teeth, ignoring the pain and reciprocating with a shot of his own. It hit one of the henchmen in the chest, and he fell to the floor in a slump. Jeremy, perhaps to no one's surprise, took off for the exit.

With a burst of desperation, mingled with adrenaline, Logan trained his gun at the other men, who would surely gun down both him and Anika. However, five men with laser guns rushed into the room and took out the rest of Simmons's men with proficiency. Logan immediately recognized one of the newcomers as Adam. He had four Core Guardsmen with him. The fifth man, who wore a high-ranking Guardsman uniform and had the same eyes as Doctor Connelly, ran toward Anika.

"Anika, are you okay?"

"Yeah, Dad."

Logan nearly groaned when he saw her sitting on the floor, leaning against her desk and nursing an arm wound. One of the laser shots had grazed her just above her elbow. He was thankful she was at least conscious. In a flash of anger, he forced himself to his feet when he saw the Core Guardsmen aim their laser guns at him. They only refrained from shooting because Adam told them to.

Adam at first seemed to care little for Logan's presence. He only had eyes for Doctor Simmons, who had backed himself into the corner near the desk, gripping the laser gun he had won back from Anika. Logan wanted the other clone to acknowledge him, to at least tell the Guardsmen to lower their weapons, but Adam's focus was on the scientist.

Adam spoke in a smooth voice. "It's over, Simmons. Tomorrow evening, the Free Army's going to enter negotiations with us. *That's* what we were celebrating today. We don't have to do this anymore; we don't have to fight."

The scientist threw Adam a contemptuous glance, ignoring Connelly Jr. and the other Guardsmen who now trained their weapons on him. He let the gun slip from his grasp just as a stream of blood flowed from his hand and splattered against the floor.

"You were my creation. A lab experiment. Who told you that you could do all this?" Simmons swooned.

Adam slipped his laser gun into a holster on his belt. "See, that's the thing...*no one* told me. I *chose* this. Isn't that what it's all about? To have the free will to choose what we want in life? And you can choose something different--let us help you, Simmons."

"It's too late." Simmons exhaled a painful breath and slumped to the ground. His eyes were still open, but the spark of life in them dimmed.

Adam looked shaken, but let out a sigh, as if relieved. Anika turned away, her father enveloping her in his arms. The Core Guardsmen lowered their weapons.

"Check the perimeter of the building, just in case any more of his men are around," Adam's deep, rich voice said. Logan, without even reflecting on it, had already moved toward Simmons.

Logan's heart pounded in his chest as he knelt over the scientist's body. He felt a lump in his throat and was torn between sorrow and pity. He stood and turned to face Adam when he approached. The other man finally acknowledged Logan.

"It's your modifications." Adam met Logan's gaze.

"Excuse me?"

"They made you more obedient, more loyal, but it wasn't perfect, was it?"

Logan glanced at Simmons one last time. His broken body just lay in the corner, a pool of blood spreading beneath him. "It was because of Logan 2. Simmons didn't have to die like this."

Adam nodded in understanding, his green eyes glinting with intelligence. "You're right, but unfortunately, he did. What is your purpose *now*, Logan?"

He shook his head. "I don't know. The furthest I got was meeting you."

Anika stood and approached him. "You can stay...help us. There's still a lot of work that needs to be done."

Connelly cleared his throat. "You may be built like Adam, but you're also your own person. Yes, I said *person.*"

Logan's sorrow and confusing emotions suddenly subsided. "So, you're not going to arrest me? I'm free to do what I want?"

Adam sized him up. "It's up to you, to live as you like, as long as you don't break any laws. You obviously can't go back to the past, and like Anika said, we still have work to do."

"I…" Logan's gaze went from Adam to Anika, then back to Adam. What if he just didn't fit in?

The other clone raised an eyebrow. A smirk played around his lips. "Anika and her father are good *friends* of mine. You can trust them."

Anika offered Logan her hand. "Are you with us?"

He took her hand in his. "Yes, I am."

***

I've recently come across several scientific articles tackling the question. Some say it's possible, and some say "you'll paradox yourself and blow up." It's all very fascinating. I have to admit, it's hard to wrap my mind around it being a possibility. Could you imagine? Who would be in control or in charge of Time Travel if it were ever possible? It sounds adventurous and amazing, but at the same time, humanity doesn't have the best track record, so we more than likely would mess some things up.

But goodness, the selfish part of me is like, "Heck yes, time travel!" because if I could do that, then I would go back and try to fix so many things from the past.

I'm a huge fan of Dr. Who, and I love the idea of time travel, going to different worlds, etc. but you know when you sit down to watch an episode, there's (often) going to be a moral to the story, or a hard decision that has to be made, wars fought, and sometimes laughter and tears. I wanted my time travel story to have a secondary layer that brings up some of the "big questions" in the context of a future world and time travel.

I couldn't tell you how I settled on my protagonist being a clone-- but it worked out great, so I won't complain.

Alesha Escobar

THE LIGHT STORM OF 2015

<u>May 3rd, 2015</u>

"Tell me we aren't flying into that?" Gina's voice shook as she grabbed Ben's arm. Ben shivered pleasurably under her warm touch.

Seated in the small cab of his dad's tiny yellow propeller plane, they faced the unbelievable display. Lights in almost every color cracked through the sky, splitting pink and purple clouds, like electrified crayon scribbles. The Light Storm was even more awe inspiring than Mr. Field, their Astronomy 101 professor, had let on. Of course, Mr. Field had never witnessed the spectacle.

No one in recorded history had ever witnessed it. The news channels had speculated about nothing else for five months straight now. The seriousness with which the media covered this story for such an extended period of time, he supposed, was a testimony to how rare and awesome it was, since the media had such a short attention span. On *The History Channel,* anthropologists discussed cave paintings and hieroglyphs that pointed to the phenomena that was now occurring before their eyes. But nothing compared to the reality of the magnificent Light Storm of 2015, nothing, that is, except the almond shaped emerald eyes of his passenger.

Ben swallowed his fear and awe, and tore his eyes from the terrifying beauty of the storm long enough to glare at his best friend. "You were the one who wanted to go back in time, Gina. Rumor is, this does it. I'm not that interested in this venture, so if you want to back out, I'll happily turn the plane around."

Ben had been trying to talk her out of it all night. He never remembered to keep his mouth shut around her. She took anything out of the ordinary as a personal challenge to fulfill her endless need for adventure. Ben wished, for the thousandth time, he hadn't related to her the time travel myth his dad told him three months ago.

"What are we waiting for, Ben? Come on." She smiled in that way he loved, her mouth pulled up at the corner, her eyes flirting.

"I don't know, Gina. I was just messing with you, telling that story. The colored lightning, or whatever it is, could mess with my electrical...I'm not sure it's safe. I mean, this plane will be like a huge conductor." Ben didn't know why he was trying to talk her out of it once her mind was made, but he had to try one more time. The colored lightning was far more wonderful than he'd imagined, but also far more terrifying.

Gina leaned into Ben, her lips a pout. Her red mouth inches from his, she whispered, "That's the point, actually. It's supposed to help *conduct* us back in time."

Ben narrowed his eyes at her lame explanation, but she ignored him.

"Please, Benjamin. Let's do it. For Bill." She leaned into him, and closed her eyes, sealing the sentence with a soft but sensual kiss. It was better than he could've imagined. Her lips tasted like the past and future.

One week earlier

Gina turned the edge of Ben's thick Astronomy 101 notebook towards her and scrawled a message in the upper right hand corner. Her jet black bangs, the only part of her pixie haircut that was long, fell into her mischievous eyes as she finished her message. She slid it to him conspiratorially, like she was still in high school and not in a huge lecture room with 300 other students. Professor Fields could care less if they passed notes all class period.

I'm so bored of this Light Storm theory shit! If Prof. Fields spends one more week on why it's important, I'm going to end myself!

Ben smiled and rolled his eyes at her. She was now miming a noose, falling into her normal, inappropriate behavior. But Ben knew she was full of crap. He could tell the Light Storm was as interesting to her as it was to the rest of the world, Professor Fields included.

When some researchers from NASA first announced the first Light Storm in more two thousand years would show itself to earth, everyone went crazy for the news. Including his dad. He remembered the text his dad sent him minutes after the announcement aired on every television, radio and online news source.

OMG. Did U jus her bout that Lgt Strm?

His dad was a horrible texter. He always used outdated abbreviations and abbreviated things that shouldn't be. And he insisted on pulling a Nellie and using the word "her" for "hear" consistently in his texts. It was actually pretty funny. Ben remembered what he texted back.

No 1 cool says OMG or knows who Nellie is anymore, Dad. Ur 2 old for that anyway. Yep I heard. Pretty cool.

His dad didn't even want to try to text his reply back. He called Ben right away and talked to him for half an hour about the theories his sci-fi online community had about the Light Storm. Ben listened impatiently, then used the excuse that he had another call so he could get off the phone with him.

His dad died three days later, a work related accident on the construction site where he was the foreman. Ben wished he had let his dad talk about his theories longer. It made him so happy. Ben never wanted to listen to his dad talk about his nerdy hobbies. His dad had wanted so much to be an astronaut as a boy, and doing the job he'd settled on to pay the bills literally ended up killing him.

Ben didn't realize he'd stopped taking notes until Gina brought a purple nail to his face, brushing away a tear he never meant to shed. He gave her a sheepish, sad smile, picked up his notebooks and quickly left the large lecture room. Professor Fields' excited conjectures on the Light Storm followed behind him.

***

Gina met him outside the men's bathroom just after Astronomy let out. She was leaning her short, curvy frame against the wall facing the bathroom. She always knew what he was up to. Living across the street from her for sixteen years probably made her the person who knew him best, apart from his parents. She walked to him, his textbook in a pile with hers. He took his Astronomy book from her with a grunted "Thanks."

"I knew you were trying to be manly and shed your tears in private, so I didn't want to bother to tell you that you left it on the table." Gina nudged him with her bony elbow. "You know, it's alright to miss your dad. I cry about him all the time. He was a riot. The nicest, nerdiest man alive. It's okay to mourn, Ben."

Ben gave her a look that said both "Thank you" and "Shut up now."

Gina stood on her tippy toes to reach her arm around his broad, lean shoulders. She smelled like lavender and mint. He loved how she never wore perfume, only oils that didn't mask the sweet scent that meant "Gina" to him.

He leaned his head on hers and mumbled, "Thanks, Gin."

She scrunched her nose and glared at him with her emeralds. She hated her nickname. He'd made it up for her their first week of college. They'd gone to a party at a Fraternity house on campus. She'd had too much gin and tonic and threw up all over his new running shoes on their walk back to the dorms. He had to throw them out. No matter how much he washed them, they still smelled like puke and pine needles.

He was walking her to her dorm now; it wasn't entirely safe on campus after about 7 p.m., even in the warmer months. She insisted, the first week of classes, she could defend herself. She probably could, but she was too cute—with her boyish haircut, lightly muscular frame, and generous hips—to walk by herself. She shouldn't have to worry about it, but shit happened on this campus.

As they passed by the poorly funded, blocky 70's style architecture of the humanities buildings, Gina poked him.

"So, what upset you?"

Ben shrugged. "My dad would've loved Mr. Fields' boring lectures on the Light Storm." Gina nodded knowingly, but waited for him to say more.

He sighed. "I was just thinking about the online theories his sci-fi group were throwing around. He was so excited about them. He was telling me about one of them, when I told him I had to get off the phone."

He paused and took a broken breath. "I didn't have to. I just didn't want to hear it. I wish he was still here. I would listen to him for hours."

When he turned to his friend to gauge her reaction, Gina had tears running down her cheeks. His heart felt a little lighter, knowing she shared a little of his pain. She never pretended to be anything she wasn't, and she loved Ben's dad. He was glad she never offered him condolences, though. They always sounded so forced and empty.

Instead, she wiped the tears from her face and prompted him, "What was the theory he was telling you about?"

Ben smiled and shook his head. "It's silly." But he thought it was a pretty cool theory, one that Gina would love. He never had fun stories. Fun stories were Gina's domain. Besides, she was looking at him, expectantly. He couldn't disappoint her.

"Well, he was saying that during the Light Storm there'll be multicolored lightning. Only it's not *really* lightning. It's supposed to be more of a colorful display, like the Aurora Borealis." Gina nodded her head. She'd heard all of this before.

But he continued, anyway, figuring she hadn't heard what he was going to next tell her. Only the biggest nerds visited the site his dad was a member of. "There's supposed to be a vortex, or something, around which this multicolored lightning swirls. The lightning, he said, isn't really like lightning at all, since it doesn't come from the earth, or the elements of our planet." He laughed lightly, knowing his voice had just raised an octave, like his father's had when he told Ben the theory. It *was* kind of cool to imagine it all.

Gina waved an impatient hand at him. "And?"

He smiled at her excitement, sliding a hand through his short, medium brown hair. He hoped, with her staring at him so intently, that he'd remembered to brush it this morning.

"Well, the nerds on this discussion board were saying that if someone were able to fly into the middle of the multicolored lightning vortex, it would allow said person to travel in time. Dad said something about the lightning enabling a person to travel through the vortex at the speed of light, without aging, or something." Ben just shook his head, noncommittally. He didn't know anything about time travel theories.

Suddenly, Gina's eyes were full of a familiar kind of mischief that made Ben quickly backtrack. "It's just a stupid online theory, Gina. Even if it were true, you could end up anywhere in time. And I don't want to be dinosaur bait, so I'm cool with our current time period."

They'd made it to the front of her dorm; a tall structure made of brick and covered with ivy. The faraway look in her eyes hadn't faded. "Yeah, maybe," she responded.

He centered his mocha brown eyes at her. "What kind of trouble are you thinking up, Gin?"

Gina shrugged her shoulders, gave him a hug goodbye and skipped up the steps to her dorm. Ben called after her, "Forget it, Gin! It's a bogus theory!"

He knew it was a bad sign when Gina stopped talking long enough to get that distant look in her eyes. She was brewing trouble. He sighed at his stupidity. He usually kept quiet. Quiet never got a man in trouble. He always regretted it when he tried to impress Gina. She'd drag him into something dumb, and because he couldn't say no to her, he'd willingly fall into it.

The night before the light storm

Ben sat in his dorm room alone. His roommate, Fin, was very social and it was a Friday night, so he had left Ben to himself only an hour after his classes were out. Ben hadn't gone out socially since his dad passed, months ago. He didn't make close friends often, though he had a lot of acquaintances. Those acquaintances tried to get him out of his grief, or to drown his sorrow with three-dollar beer, but his refusal and consistently morose attitude soon scared them off.

Only Gina stuck around no matter how shitty his attitude was. He hadn't heard from her tonight, so he moped around his dorm, looking at pictures of his dad and watching old horror movies, while the rest of the CU celebrated the weekend.

A knock sounded on his door. He smiled. Only one person ever showed up unannounced. He jumped up from his ugly, brown second-hand couch, and opened the door, grinning. "Hey, Gin."

She stuck her tongue out at Ben. She'd changed her tongue ring to the one with the eight-ball on the end. He had bought it for her twentieth birthday; she'd always been a superstitious person. She loved it and wore it almost as often as the shamrock one. She bumped his skinny frame out of the doorway with her hip and lifted her right hand in triumph.

"I brought refreshments! What kind of moping are we doing tonight?" She looked over her shoulder at Ben, who had been gawking at the black leggings that hugged her bounteous butt.

"Eyes up, perv!" She winked at him in a way that said she didn't really mind the look and set the twelve pack of Blue Moon, their favorite beer, on the makeshift coffee table, a tractor tire with a round piece of glass placed on top.

Ben hurriedly cleared the couch of the pictures of his dad. He swept them back into their shoebox. Gina rummaged through the kitchen cabinets, looking for a couple of clean glasses. She sighed and began washing a couple dirty ones. Her search for something clean had come up empty handed.

"Your place is a pit, Ben. I remember when you used to be clean." Her voice was playful, so Ben ignored her and slid the shoebox under the couch with his foot.

"There are oranges in the fridge, Gin." He cleared off the immediate area. She was right. The place was a pit. He hadn't cared about cleaning up, lately.

"Found 'em!" She walked out of the kitchen with sliced oranges and two clean glasses.

Ben took the glasses and set them on the tire table, filling them with beer and putting an orange in each, while Gina made herself comfortable on the now clean couch.

"Which movie is this?" She asked, offhandedly. "I know we've watched it before, but I have a hard time remembering the names of the old ones."

Ben wanted to tell her she had a hard time remembering her own last name most days, but he just smiled at her with a raised eyebrow. She flipped him off, knowing what he was thinking. He answered her question, belatedly, "It's *House on Haunted Hill.*"

"Ah, I see. One of Bill's favorite's, right?" She looked at him with a mixture of sympathy and frustration.

Ben flinched at the mention of his dad's name. He nodded as he took a long pull from his drink. Gina took a sip of hers and picked up the remote and turned the television off.

"It's one of those nights, is it?" she asked.

Ben shrugged and took another drink of his beer.

Gina sighed. "I know you miss him and want to remember him, but, correct me if I'm wrong, these evening-long remembrance sessions tend to leave you a little depressed in the end, no?"

Ben gulped his beer before answering. "I don't want to forget him. I want to remember everything I can. And I feel like..." He stopped, embarrassed.

Gina leaned in, her face intent. "You feel like what?"

Ben exhaled. "I can't remember what he smelled like or looked like, sometimes. I don't remember the sound of his voice some days, and it's only been a couple of months. What happens when it's been years? I don't want to forget him, Gin." His stomach protested the beer he'd just gulped. It'd been in knots ever since his dad passed.

Gina sipped her beer before answering. "He smelled like sawdust most of the time." She grinned, and Ben laughed quietly.

"Yeah, he did. And menthol cigarettes." He smiled at her and she leaned back, nodding, closing her eyes pensively for a short moment before opening them and leaning towards him, her body excited.

"Actually, I came here on a mission, one that might help you have fun *and* remember Bill." Her eyes sparkled impishly.

"Oh yeah, what's that?" Ben eyed her warily, his tone accusing.

She leaned in, her short frame abuzz with excitement. "Well, you know that theory he told you about? I looked it up, and it actually seems like these people really researched this Light Storm and the science behind it. It sounds pretty legitimate. And, even better, there's a consensus in the community that says if a person goes into the vortex and concentrates solely on one specific date when they reach the wormhole, that's the date they'll be brought back to." She bounced on her knees, grinning widely.

Ben began to argue the logic of what she was saying, but she held up a finger to stifle it. "I'm not done. The Light Storm Time Travelers Community also suggests a person's presence in the said time dimension will be very temporary, and they'll eventually be transported back into their own time to balance the continuum. I mean, wouldn't that be great? You would go to this other place in time, and then, BAM! You'd be back home." She grinned from ear to ear, looking like an adorable imp.

Ben finished his first beer and was filling his glass with a second. The heavy sadness of missing his father was being replaced by a pleasant, warm buzz. "That *would* be cool. If it wasn't a totally bogus theory. Which it is."

Gina huffed impatiently. "Look, I know it's probably some really well composed geek drivel that I should ignore, but I can't. I've got a feeling on this one, Benjamin."

Oh, no. One of Gina's feelings. That always meant trouble. When Gina had a feeling about something, she would do her damnedest to see it through. It was part of her superstitious nature. She believed these "feelings" were spiritually inspired. Ben sighed heavily and downed half of his beer.

Gina took his silence as permission to continue, which she enthusiastically did. "I've thought a lot about this. If we did go back in time, we couldn't mess with history, like, *big* history. We couldn't stop someone from being assassinated, for example. We don't know what that would do to us, if it would erase our very being. So we have to stay away from that. But if we just changed something minor in our *own* lives, then that couldn't hurt. Also, about half of the Time Travelers Community believe a person can only traverse in the same time as their own bodily being. I'm not so sure, but better safe than sorry."

Before Ben could tell her there was no way in hell he was flying into an electrical storm on the tenuous time travel theories of bored geeks, Gina scooted closer to him. Blood flew to his cheeks and his head swam. She opened his right hand. Just when he thought she was going to shove their friendship onto the next level, she slapped a piece of scribbled on paper into it and hopped back to her original seat.

Ben's head was still swimming from the beer and her proximity. He looked at the small piece of torn out notebook paper. It read: 11/12/2013 2:00 p.m.

"What's this?" He asked her, confused and slightly tipsy.

Gina's smile made her look a bit like a mad scientist. "The day I got in the accident and broke my leg. It ruined my chances to be a swimmer on scholarship. I had Ivy League schools looking into me before that day. I couldn't swim my whole senior year, and you know I've been less coordinated since then." Ben nodded. She walked with a little limp since the accident. Her leg never healed properly.

Gina's face was forlorn as she thought about lost possibilities. "If not for that, I might be in some fancy school. No tuition or loans to worry about. I could study to be a doctor on someone else's dime."

Ben couldn't help but smile ruefully at the hopeful gleam in his best friend's eyes. He knew this was always in the back of Gina's mind. That day had been devastating for her. Though their university had a swim team and competed, it wasn't the focus of their sports program, which, like most state schools, was football. She continually won her swim meets hands down, though even with the injury. She wanted to study medicine, and swimming was her chance to go to the schools that mattered. He knew being stuck in a state school had smashed something inside of her. Just like losing his dad crushed him, though, admittedly, to a lesser degree.

She finished off her second beer with a belch and a blush. She played with the label on one of the empty beer bottles on the tire table, and Ben saw the hurt she was trying to hide. "Look, Ben. I know this theory is probably nothing. But what if there's something to it after all? Wouldn't it be the best way to remember the nerdiest man alive? We've both been down in the dumps. I just feel like this is going to change that."

He shook his head, "I don't know, Gina. I mean, it's really dangerous..."

Gina cut him off before he could voice any more opposition. "I know, I know. But you can fly. I know you still fly your grandpa's old crop duster your dad trained you on. You're a pro with it." She scooted closer to him.

"Remember my sixteenth birthday?" she asked him, shyly.

How could he forget? For her sixteenth birthday, Ben's dad gave him permission to take her in the plane and do a circle around grandpa's farm. Gina was elated, having wanted to fly in the plane ever since she learned that Ben could operate it. She got so excited when they took off, that she went to grab Ben's arm and accidentally grabbed his crotch. For her, it was the most awkward thing that had ever happened to her. She apologized profusely, her face a vibrant scarlet, and tried to forget it immediately.

For Ben, it was the highlight of his entire year, and certainly the highlight of the night, which was, actually, pretty awesome apart from that. They were able to watch the sun go down on the Midwestern horizon from the air. He imagined the sunset was what Gina referred to now, but Ben still thought of it as the night Gina grabbed his crotch.

"I *can* fly. I *was* trained well. I was also trained *not* to fly into lightning storms, Gin." He looked up at her. He wished he hadn't. She was pouting. A fake, cute pout, the one Ben couldn't say no to.

"Please, Ben. We can just take the plane up there, and we don't have to fly near it, if you think it's too dangerous."

Ben was about to object again, before Gina stopped him dead with four words: "It could be romantic."

Her eyes were serious, which almost never happened. She slid her hand onto the top of his, and his body responded immediately, instantly sobering. He bit his lip and nodded slightly. "Okay, you win. We can go *watch* it, at least."

Gina was jubilant. She poured them each another beer and danced around the tire table. "Yay!" She ruffled his already messy hair. "Just in case, memorize that date! I'm going to Harvard, bitches!"

Ben shook his head, knowing that he may have just signed his death warrant, but he only said, "Gina, I'm the only one here, besides you, and I'm not a bitch."

The night of the Light Storm

When they drove up to his grandpa's farm in Ben's old Ford Escort and pulled into the drive, Gina almost jumped out of her seat.

"What *is* that?" She pointed to the 'For Sale' sign in front of the large, bright yellow farm house that had been in his father's family for over one hundred years.

She glared at Ben. "When were you going to tell me that Patty and Benny were selling the farm?"

Ben sighed. "Dad and mom were helping with the payments. We can't afford to do that without Dad's paycheck. We tried. I even worked extra hours bailing hay for Mr. Murray on Sunday afternoons, but it only bought them time to pack. Mom's job *just* takes care of our mortgage and bills for the house in Des Moines."

His mom was a community college Geology instructor. His dad's construction company was very successful before he passed, but it was not something Ben was trained to take over, so his uncle Geoff had taken it on and promised to hire him out of school, after Ben earned his business degree. Ben always wanted to help his dad with the company, but it seemed a sad prospect with him gone.

His throat caught. "The plane's for sale, too. Though, grandpa isn't sure it's going to bring much to relieve their finances. He said we could take it out tonight, though. They're having dinner with mom in Des Moines right now."

Gina fought the tears back as she sat next to him, her full lips quivering, so he didn't say anything else. She broke her silence when they pulled up to the small hanger that housed the plane. "I should've asked. I feel like an ass, not knowing any of this."

Ben shook his head. "It is what it is. There's nothing your knowing could do to change it."

Gina shrugged, "Maybe, but I should've been better about asking, anyway. I miss your dad so much, not as much as you miss him, I know, but it's been hard for me to bring it up. I never knew my dad, but I never felt like I missed out. Not with Bill always around making sure I knew how to change tires, coming to my swim meets, and glowering at any boys who came calling for me. I haven't been back here since winter break."

She wiped away a single tear as it slid down her dark cheek and shook her head. "I'm sorry. It was selfish of me not to ask more about what's going on."

Ben just smiled at her, touched by her love for his father. "No. It's alright. I don't like talking about all that's going wrong. It doesn't fix it. I could have told you. I just didn't see the point."

They got out of the car and walked quietly to the old yellow propeller plane. Ole Yeller, as his dad called it. Ben helped Gina into the co-pilot's side of the plane, as she was short and it was a fairly tall hop, and her leg was a little bum. But he also got to put his hands on her waist this way, which was, really, his ulterior motive.

When she was seated, she smiled down at him. "You're pretty strong for someone so skinny."

Ben shook his head at her and walked around to the pilot's side of the plane. He hopped gracefully into the pilot's seat and buckled his restraints. Gina was expertly buckling her own. She'd been his co-pilot for years now. He looked over at his silly best friend. Her excitement was returning with their adventure in sight. The Light Storm would start just as dark fell, any minute now.

Ben turned the ignition and tingled as the engine sputtered to life. The vibration of the old plane shook him to his bones, making him feel alive. He inched the plane forward to get free of the hanger. He steered it towards the makeshift runway that would be their vantage point for the Light Storm.

**

"I don't know, Gina. I was just messing with you, telling that story. The colored lightning, or whatever it is, could mess with my electrical...I'm not sure it's safe. I mean, this plane will be like a huge conductor." Ben didn't know why he was trying to talk her out of it once her mind was made, but he had to try one more time. The colored lightning was far more wonderful than he'd imagined, but also far more terrifying.

Gina leaned into Ben, her lips a pout. Her red mouth inches from his, she whispered, "That's the point, actually. It's supposed to help *conduct* us back in time."

Ben narrowed his eyes at her lame explanation, but she ignored him.

"Please, Benjamin. Let's do it. For Bill." She leaned into him, and closed her eyes, sealing the sentence with a soft but sensual kiss. It was better than he could've imagined. Her lips tasted like the past and future.

Ben's head spun, his thoughts still full of her soft, sweet kiss. He turned the key to the ignition and his dad's plane sputtered to life again. He steered onto the runway, gaining speed. As they got closer to the storm, he glanced at Gina. Her almond eyes screamed adventure. Her hand reached for his leg, just like they were sixteen again. Only this time, she hit her mark and squeezed his leg until it hurt, but he barely registered the pain over his excitement. His heart skipped a beat, and it had little to do with the speed at which he was traveling down the bumpy runway. He realized in that moment he would do anything for the woman next to him.

The small plane lifted and headed toward the swirling mass of glowing squiggles, miles ahead of them. The brilliant display he was flying into was blindingly beautiful, but he found himself unable to keep his eyes on his destination. As they gained altitude and flew toward the glittering unknown of the Light Storm, Ben realized he was in love. He hoped he lived long enough to enjoy it. Just as the thought hit him, the small plane started shaking violently.

He glanced over at Gina, his fear reflected in her eyes. "I'm going to turn it around, Gin. This is too dangerous."

Gina nodded sadly but resolutely, finally in agreement. The

colored lightning was at least a half mile away, but as Ben tried to steer the plane away from the neon pinks, oranges, greens and yellows of the storm, the jagged forms of lightning shot out towards the small propeller plane and wrapped their electric arms around it.

Ben and Gina's hair stood on end. Ben prepared himself for the eventual shock of the lightning, but he didn't feel the jolting pain he expected. He cranked the rudder of the plane, one more time as hard as he could. Too hard, it broke off in his hand. He went to call out, but caught Gina mouthing something at him over the din of the shaking plane, and he swallowed his yelp.

"Twelve, Twelve, Two-Thousand Fourteen. Eight a.m.!" She screamed at the top of her lungs. He frowned at her, confused and terrified.

"Twelve, Twelve, Two-Thousand Fourteen. Eight a.m.! Say it!" she yelled.

Ben had tears in his eyes. He had no idea why she thought the stupid theory was still going to work. They were going to die, and he hadn't told her yet how he felt. But he always listened to Gina, even when he shouldn't.

"Twelve, Twelve, Two-Thousand Fourteen. Eight a.m.!" He sobbed. He didn't realize in his panic that the date they were both yelling, as if their lives or deaths depended on it, wasn't the date of Gina's accident.

The colored lightning surrounded the plane, escaping into its metal corners and seeping into the cab. It made a deafening buzz. The light clung to them like skinny, neon leeches, but it didn't electrocute them. Instead, the lightning felt like puffs of icy air as it soaked into the pores of their skin. They were quickly losing body heat, becoming filled with an icy vapor. Ben chanced a look ahead. He realized they were being pulled into a dark, endless tunnel of sorts, so black that it made him feel the frightening jolt of momentary blindness.

He looked away from the dark void. His stomach churned. Acid burned his throat. He looked at Gina one more time. He would fill his remaining minutes with her face. She was still screaming the date so loud that her voice was breaking. She grabbed his hand, frantically, and squeezed it until he felt like they were joined as one, glowing neon being.

"Say it, Ben!"

Ben had stopped yelling the date, in his terror, but nodded and began shouting again, as loud as he could. "Twelve, Twelve, Two-Thousand Fourteen. Eight a.m.!"

Suddenly, they were enveloped in darkness. Ben and Gina were gently falling apart, a million tiny pieces. Before their voices were sucked into the void, Gina bellowed, "Twelve, Twelve, Two-Thousand Fourteen. Eight a.m. I've always loved you, Ben!"

Ben wanted to tell her he loved her too, only her, but he could no longer see or hear her, or see or hear *anything*. Just after her proclamation, Ben heard a sound like a giant squid tentacle pulling against a pane of glass. Then there was nothing but the void.

12/12/2014 8.a.m

Ben felt like he was severely hung over when he woke. He cracked open a stubborn eye and willed his stiff, sore body to turn to the right. If he were able to, he'd have bolted upright. This was his bedroom, his home in Des Moines, not his dorm. Did he and Gina make it out of the storm alive? Where was she?

Ben carefully sat up, forcing his body to move. It felt like he was dream walking. Every movement slowed and required concentrated effort to carry out. He laid a cold hand on his nightstand and grasped for the place he normally kept his phone. He felt it, but had a hard time gripping it. He felt like a poltergeist, inhabiting a body not quite his own. He focused his whole body on the task of picking up his phone. He was finally able to hold it, clumsily, in his hand. It took him another five minutes to unlock the display to read the time, but this shattered the concentration and the phone clattered to the bedroom floor.

His phone always displayed the date and time in bold on a neon green background, and the glowing screen read: 12/12/2014 8:05 a.m. He blinked his eyes with some effort and looked at the phone on the floor, just to make sure. Sure enough, it read 12/12/2014 8:06 a.m. They had done it! Gina was right. But why this date? Why not the date she injured herself?

Now that Ben wasn't worried about dying, it took him very little effort to put two and two together. They went about four months back in time. While he never concentrated on the date his dad died, he was sure it was something Gina would've remembered. She always thought about life in a series of dates. Ben thought of life in a series of moments. Gina had brought him back four hours before his dad died. He remembered the time of his dad's death because he was on lunch break from his job down the street at the deli, when the police came to the door.

Gina wanted to save his father, to *do it for Bill*. That's what she had said, now it all made sense. She'd intended this all along. She just hadn't wanted to bum him out by mentioning the date of his father's death. He could kiss her. If he knew where she was...

Panic gripped him. What if he made it and she didn't? What if she was lost somewhere in the void? He decided to try to think about this crazy situation as logically as he could. If future Ben was thrust into his past body, into the place his past body occupied during Winter Break, then future Gina would be in the same time and place her past body occupied. She had to be.

That meant Gina should be next door; she was home that day. She'd come over after he heard the news about his dad, and she had stayed with him for two days straight. *Of course* she'd choose this date! Ben was an idiot for thinking she'd do anything else.

He took a deep breath and forced his heavy legs over the side of his bed. He found if he thought of his body as a suit of armor (which was pretty much what it felt like), he could get it to do what he wanted it to. He stood and walked to the front door of his house, just down the hall from his room, and only knocked one picture down from the wall in the process. He tried to be quiet, but he was trying equally hard not to take this past-present body and go to his parents' room. His dad would be waking up to get ready for work.

He couldn't talk well in this form of himself. He knew he had to get his father to stay home without interacting with him. He felt, in every fiber of his being, it would be disastrous if his father saw him. He opened their bright red front door and walked out of the house into the cold December morning.

Huge icicles hung from the rafters of the single-story house. That's right. It was icy that day. That's why the crane operator had a hard time controlling the load he carried. That's why, when he put the brakes on the crane, it skidded to a halt, its load coming unbalanced. That's why a steel beam had fallen from the load and crushed his dad's truck, the truck where his dad had been eating his lunch.

He was so lost in his horrible reverie that he didn't notice the door across the street swing open. He didn't see Gina mechanically approach him from her house, a smile plastered on her face. And he certainly didn't catch the two kitchen knives clutched carefully in her hands. When he looked up, she was almost across the street.

If he could have cried out in joy, in this form, he would have. Instead, he walked toward her, one lead step at a time, and met her by his dad's old work truck, the truck that was supposed to be crushed with him inside it. Ben laid a steely hand on the truck and worked up a smile. If the truck was whole, so was his dad.

Gina, unable to speak, lifted her right arm and motioned that he should take a knife. He must have been able to frown his confusion, because she rigidly knelt down and placed the needle sharp fillet knife to his father's truck tire. She slowly punctured it before sliding it down the length of the tire. She looked at him and gave him a slow motion thumbs up. Ben took the other knife from her hand, and with the same slow, measured movements, moved to the front of his dad's truck to puncture the two front tires.

They worked as quickly as their fogged bodies would allow, both of them knowing his dad would be out of the house at 8:45 a.m. on the dot. He was a creature of habit. Ben surmised Gina was trying to do enough damage to keep his dad out of work for a few hours. This would do it. He had only one spare tire at home, and two tires were already ragged and deflated.

Ben and Gina made the cuts long enough so that no patch would fix the tire, which ensured his dad would need to call someone to come out and fix the truck. This kind of job would take hours, and mom had already left for work. Gina really knew his dad. He wouldn't call someone to pick him up. He was fastidious about his truck. He'd get it fixed that day, and he'd hover around the vehicle until the repairs were done.

When they were done with the tires, they both rose stiffly. Gina motioned with a heavy arm to follow her. She walked away from the truck toward his house. Ben followed her. How, by now, could he not trust she knew what to do better than he did? She crouched just at the corner of his house, and he settled himself behind her, just as the door to his house opened.

There, walking at a normal speed to his truck, was Ben's dad. If his body would've allowed it, Ben would've run to him, but Gina turned, her eyes full of hope, and mouthed, "No." She felt it too. His dad shouldn't see them like this. He settled himself back behind her, in a crouch, but he stared in awe at his lanky, curly headed father as if he was Michelangelo's *David*. He willed himself to memorize the burnished brown of his hair, sprinkled with gray, the laugh lines at the sides of his mouth, and the almost black eyes, narrowing in anger.

His father immediately registered that his tires were demolished. He looked around for a heated second before cussing, "Damn neighborhood kids! I bet it was that William's boy."

Ben laughed on the inside. His father had a running beef with the kid down the street, who was always scuffing up the sidewalks with his skateboard and rolling over his dad's flower bed. Ben felt a little bad that the kid would probably be reamed for something he didn't do, but only a little.

Ben held his breath as his dad retrieved his cell phone from his Philip's Contracting jacket. He punched some numbers in angrily. Someone must have picked up, because he started talking in a rushed voice. "Yeah, Frank, I need you to oversee the guys today. Some idiot ruined my truck tires. I bet it was that damn punk kid, Fret, or Bret— or whatever the hell his name is. Uh, huh. Okay. Yeah, I probably won't be in until after one. The tires are trashed. Okay. Well, thanks, man. It'll be good overtime for you. You know I wouldn't ask if I didn't need it. Okay. Thanks again. Bye."

Ben's heart soared. His frustrated father kicked the ruined tire of his truck, muttering about 'punks who have no respect for other people's property.' Ben's borrowed body started to feel lighter. He smiled at his best friend, who was giving him a thumbs up, when his dad started walking their way. Shit! They had to move, fast, but that was impossible. They couldn't really hope for much more than a snail's pace in their borrowed past shells. In slow motion, Gina threw herself at Ben, and before he could fall to the ground, their hands met and their future atoms merged again. Ben heard another loud sucking sound and was forced back into nothingness.

May 11th 2015 11 p.m.

"Benjamin Kurt Philip! Wake up, right now! If you don't wake up, I'll...I'll..." The voice floating above the nothingness faltered and broke into sobs. "Oh, God. Bring my son back to me, please. *Please.*"

A feeling of lightness settled on Ben, the tingling sense of blood, muscle and bones filled his being again. His eyes fluttered against the darkness and opened without ceremony. His reactions were not stilted and robotic, though they *were* painful.

"Dad?" Ben's voice was hoarse, as if he hadn't used it in a very long time. The blurred figure above him was taking the shape of a man whose form Ben thought would never grace the earth again. The shaggy hair, black-brown eyes and lean frame hovered over him. Seldom shed tears streamed down his face.

"Benny! You're awake." His dad, who never cried, started openly sobbing and aggressively kissing Ben's face.

The Ben who hadn't lost his dad would have protested, but this Ben knew what it meant to feel his dad's rough cheek against his own. He gratefully accepted the sloppy affection. Ben breathed the scent of woodchips and menthol cigarettes. He felt as if his heart might burst from happiness. *My dad's alive!* He studied his dad's face with an intensity he knew made Bill uncomfortable.

"Hi, Dad. I missed you so much." His voice broke and tears ran down his cheek.

His dad frowned at him, confused at his response, but sputtered out, "Hey, it's alright, Benny!" He wiped the tears from his son's face and then put a sleeve to his own eyes.

"It's only been a few days, but I missed you too. We were afraid it was a concussion, but the doctors said they thought your body was just taking the time it needed to heal. Now I'll have to apologize for telling them they didn't know shit." His dad smiled sheepishly and gently laid his hand on Ben's head, patting his son affectionately.

Ben tried to sit up, but a sharp pain stabbed his sides. He groaned in agony. His dad gently pushed him back down, "Whoa there, man, you have three broken ribs. You're not going to be able to sit well for a few days, at least. That business with the plane," he shook his head in exasperation, "that was nuts, son. What were you two doing? I thought you just wanted to see the Lights, not get electrocuted. I should have never told you that theory, and why did you tell Gina? You know how she is! Me and my big mouth."

Ben almost tried to jump up again, but corrected himself. He settled for shifting his head from side to side and vainly searching for his best friend. "Gina! Where is she?! Is she okay?"

His father laid a patient hand on his arm. "Just a second, son."

Bill frowned and left the room, leaving Ben to panic. Why had he left? Was he bringing his mom in to give him bad news? His dad was terrible about giving bad news. Gina hadn't made it. It was his fault. His heart sank to his stomach and he felt violently nauseous. What would life be like with his dad at home, but no Gina to share it with?

But almost as quickly as his dad left, the door to his room opened again. "Alright, son, your sister can visit with you for a few minutes, alright? But then the doctors want to talk to you. Your mom ran home to shower, I just called her and she's on her way back."

Ben was so confused. He was an only child. Did he and Gina change the outcome of his life that drastically? He couldn't see how...Then she was standing above him, emerald eyes, short black hair, light brown skin, and a fresh bandage plastered on the side of her head. Of course. He was in the hospital. Only family could visit very sick patients. His heart thumped like it was going to come free of his chest. The way he looked at Gina must have alerted his dad to their need for privacy, because he backed out of the room with an excuse that he needed coffee.

Ben lifted his hand, reaching towards his father. His heart lurched. What if his dad left the room and never came back again? What if this was a dream? His eyes filled with tears. Gina took the hand that was stretched out toward his father. "It's okay, Benjamin. He's real. He's here. He'll be back." Her eyes shone with tears. "We did it."

Ben smiled and breathed deeply, which was actually fairly painful. He winced. "Gina. I thought you didn't make it. What you planned, I mean, it was crazy, but it was..." he struggled to find the right word, "beautiful. You *saved* my dad. What about Harvard?"

Gina rolled her eyes. "Actually, besides a bump on the head and a few bruises, I faired pretty well. The plane didn't, unfortunately." She grimaced, and he sighed. *Poor Ole Yeller.*

She shrugged. "As for Harvard, they don't deserve me." She fluffed her short hair dramatically. "Anyway," she leaned down and kissed Ben lightly on the mouth, "CU has its perks, and Cambridge is so far away."

Ben knew his face was probably a deep crimson, but he didn't care. He wouldn't regret words unsaid. Life was too short. Even with what they did to bring his dad back, life was never guaranteed to be anything other than fleeting. He wouldn't waste any more time waiting for good things to come to him. He knew his one chance to fix the past had been used. From now on, it was all forward.

He met his best friend's earnest gaze, "I've always loved you, Gina."

Her eyes shone so brightly, they rivaled the Light Storm.

***

I am a part of a wonderful Google+ social community called Geekscapes. In this community, our moderator shares daily pictures from some of the most talented geek artists of today. Our community has many avid sci-fi and fantasy geeks who write stories about some of the pictures, myself included.

Ben and Gina's story started as a mini tale about a lovely piece of art that showed a yellow crop duster facing a brilliant display of swirling lights. After writing what is now the first four paragraphs of my short story, my fellow Google+ geeks democratically decided that I was not done by tagging me several times asking, "What happens next, +H.M.Jones?" I tend to listen to my geek friends' insights, so I figured out what happened next for this anthology.

H.M. Jones

END OF THE ROAD

The oversized painting featuring a wide dirt road, bordered by towering trees in full bloom, had hung for decades above the sofa in Nell Henry's living room. Today, her two daughters-in-law stood before the framed piece of art and one commented, "Mother Henry, you really should take the painting to Antique Roadshow."

"I agree," said the other. "It looks very old. It could be worth a mint."

Nell laughed. "Afraid not! I bought it at a starving artists' sale. I thought its perspective would make this narrow room look bigger."

She remembered that day clearly. The artist was a nervous type, her eyes darted back and forth as she asked if Nell was certain she wanted to buy it. Her odd line of questioning made Nell suspect she'd decided not to sell it, but the woman was adamant that wasn't the reason. The artist said two others had purchased the painting, but both had returned it. Now that Nell stood gazing at the artwork, she wondered if it had something to do with how large the painting was.

Nell lowered her voice to a whisper. "She told me when the buyers took the painting home, they said it made them feel weird. Then she muttered something about how she felt 'captive' when she painted it, as if someone else held the brushes."

Naturally, she had scoffed at that nonsense and paid for the painting. It hung there for over thirty years. *She* had never experienced anything strange when looking at it. In fact, she thought about replacing it with something more contemporary, but something about it made her hold on to the painting.

Nell's granddaughter, five-year-old Madison Henry, or "Maddie," had been listening in on their conversation. She squeezed herself with glee. Grandma wouldn't sell the painting to those men on television. Whenever she slipped away from her big sister and cousins, she'd go into the living room to gaze into the painting. The trees grew smaller and the road became narrower. She wondered what was at the end of the road.

Sometimes, when she'd stand in front of it, Maddie imagined she was looking out a big window. Then she'd whirl around and look out the real window. Outside, houses and cars filled the view. When Maddie spun back, she saw all those beautiful trees and the road that begged to be followed. Sometimes she'd lie on her back on the sofa and hear bunnies hopping in the grass under the trees, see squirrels burying nuts, and birds flying through the trees. If she moved to the other end of the sofa, she might see a dog run down the road or a cat slowly cross it. If she stood on the couch, which, of course, she wasn't supposed to, Maddie could press her cheek against the painting and hear birds chirping. Once, she even heard the sound of children playing.

One day Maddie stood on the back of the sofa, and she lifted her right foot up and placed it on the road. She almost put her left on there too, but she heard grandma coming. Embarrassed, she quickly got down from the couch and ran to give grandma a big hug.

The next time Maddie was alone in the living room, she put both feet on the road and began to walk. Walking! She actually walked right into the picture, and it scared her to pieces. She quickly backed up and landed feet first on the sofa. Grandma came in at that moment and frowned.

"Maddie, I'm surprised at you. You know sofas aren't trampolines."

Madison lowered her gaze. "Sorry." Then she quickly glanced up to see if the painting showed her footprints. It looked fine. *Maybe I just imagined it,* Maddie thought. But even at her young age, Maddie knew it was too real to be a dream. She had walked a little way down the road. Now, more than ever, she wanted to walk to the end.

Months later, right after turning six, Madison felt brave enough to try to walk into the painting again. The perfect opportunity came when her parents went away on a trip with her aunt and uncle. All of the Henry granddaughters stayed at Grandma's. Maddie waited until everyone else watched Disney movies on Grandma's old VCR in the den. Maddie climbed on the back of the sofa and walked into the painting.

She had been walking quite a distance when a hand grabbed her shoulder. "What do you think *you're* doing, Miss Mindy Lou? Look at those funny clothes! Seems to me like you're running away," said the woman with a voice that reminded Maddie of her mom's favorite movie, Scarlet and the Wind, or something like that.

What? Maddie felt completely confused. *Why is this weird talking woman calling me Mindy Lou? Why did she say my clothes, just jeans and a t-shirt, look funny?* She looked back at the African American woman, who looked a lot like Miss Russell, her first grade teacher whom she adored. But unlike Miss Russell, who always wore pretty clothes and had a fancy hair style, this woman wore a long black dress with a big white apron over it, and her hair was bound in a blue kerchief *And she says my clothes look funny*, thought Maddie as she tried to wiggle out of the woman's grip.

"Not so fast, Missy. Just because your folks aren't here, don't mean you can get by with anything. I'm taking you back to Miss Schill."

She swung Madison around and headed toward the biggest house the little girl had ever seen. It was white and across the front had a large porch with a bunch of tall, fat poles going across. The woman marched Madison inside and up a wide flight of shiny stairs to a room where three little blonde, blue-eyed girls chattered as they worked on something with needles and colorful thread. They looked up at Maddie and giggled.

"Where's Miss Schill?" demanded Maddie's captor.

One of the girls, who looked quite a bit like Madison, piped up. "Flora, don't you remember? She's giving Miss Cynthia a lesson on the pianoforte."

The woman's eyes widened as she looked from the speaker to Maddie. "You're Mindy Lou. Who are you?"

In a quiet voice, Maddie answered, "I'm Madison Henry."

"Oh, you're a Henry cousin."

Maddie listened as all three girls began to talk at once. Not one denied she was her cousin! Maddie figured this might turn out to be fun. At that point, the governess, Miss Schill, came to investigate the commotion. Recently, the master of the plantation, Mr. Henry, had hired her to care for Miss Cynthia and Miss Mindy Lou and to help Cynthia with her piano lessons. Last night, Master Henry's brother and wife had arrived from their plantation. Their plan, Miss Schill learned, was to leave their girls also in her care while the four adults traveled to Atlanta for an auction.

Maddie heard Miss Schill's almost inaudible murmur. "I thought there were only two cousins, but here's a third who looks like all the others but dressed like one of the little slave boys in blue pants, like broadcloth, and an odd white shirt. Poor thing. She's probably been hiding away in the slave quarters since yesterday." Miss Schill stepped to the dresser, opened a drawer, grabbed a thin white dress like the others wore, and handed it to Maddie.

Miss Schill returned to Cynthia's lesson. Madison shrugged and changed her clothes. All eyes were on her, and the little girls gasped when they saw her "Hello, Kitty" underwear. Maddie rolled her eyes and sat down. One of the girls handed her some embroidery work. Maddie, who had never held a needle before, tried to mimic the others' needlework. They whispered to each other and laughed at this curious girl's clumsy efforts. Not one to cry easily, Maddie held back her tears.

The girl who looked like her, Mindy Lou, laid down her embroidery and put her arm around Maddie, "It's all right. It's near time for dinner."

As the ice broke, the girls clustered around Maddie and started to ask her questions.

"Who are you, really?" asked one.

"I'm really Madison Henry, but you can call me Maddie."

"How did you get here?"

"I just walked down the road."

"Oh, are you from the next plantation?"

"No, I'm from down the road."

"You act different. I don't think you're from around here," Mindy Lou scoffed.

Miss Schill interrupted. "Time to get ready to eat." The governess poured water from the pitcher into a bowl for the girls to wash their hands. Maddie whispered to Mindy Lou that she had to go to the bathroom. That word confused Mindy Lou, but she figured it out and showed Maddie another bowl to squat over.

As they walked down to the kitchen, Mindy Lou commented, "I

hope you just had to make water. Flora says we're old enough to go to the outhouse to do our big business."

Maddie wrinkled up her nose as she remembered using an outhouse, once on a camping trip. Just then, they reached the kitchen. Maddie had never seen anything like it. No refrigerator and no microwave, just a big black stove and a wooden table with benches. Dinner was bowls of something yellow called mush with milk. Seeing Maddie's look of distaste, Mindy Lou explained, "When Father and Mother are here, we eat in the dining hall. We have meat and sauce with hot biscuits, and greens and pie for dessert. While they're gone, Cook is lazy"

Maddie tried a spoonful of mush and began to gag. Mindy Lou looked offended. "It's not that bad. Put some sorghum on it." Maddie didn't like it any better with the sweet, dark brown syrup. Curious about Maddie's distaste, Mindy Lou asked what she usually ate.

"Pizza rolls, chicken nuggets, and I eat tacos and mac and cheese."

Mindy Lou had no idea what these things were, but said, "They sound terrible."

Maddie started to argue but stopped herself, "What do we do after this?"

"We take a nap."

Maddie looked shocked. "Naps are for babies."

"Maybe where you come from, but here everyone naps. It's too hot to do anything else." Maddie dutifully lay down for a nap, but as soon as the other girls were sleeping, she got out of bed. She looked out the window and there was the road. It was time to escape this crazy place and go back to Grandma's.

Mindy Lou had only pretended to sleep and saw Maddie creep toward the door. She shifted and whispered to Maddie, "Do you like kittens?"

Maddie's eyes lit up. "Yes."

"There are some new ones in the hayloft. If we're quiet, we can sneak out there."

Soon, the two girls sat in the loft, each petting a kitten so tiny that one finger spanned the space between its miniature ears.

Bonding with her look-alike over the irresistible kittens, Maddie asked, "How old are you?"

"I'm eight, going on nine."

Maddie was surprised. They were the same size. With her sixth birthday just this past week, she announced, "I'm nearly seven."

With that settled, they went on to other topics. Maddie was curious about all the African American people working in the fields out the loft window. "Who are they?" she asked Mindy Lou.

"They're slaves. Don't you know anything?'

"What are slaves?'

"My father, he's master of the plantation, buys them. They work for him."

Maddie's eyes grew round in disbelief. "Buys people? *Nobody* buys people!"

"Yes, they do. We need a lot of people to work the plantation."

"Does your dad, I mean father, pay them lots of money?"

"No, he doesn't pay them anything, and he whips them if they don't work." Mindy Lou pointed to a horsewhip hanging on a peg on the barn wall below them."

Maddie couldn't believe her ears. Enraged she asked, "Why?"

"Because. They're not like us."

"You said I'm not like you either."

A mean look came over Mindy Lou's face. Her eyes shifted from blue to a greenish-yellow. "You'd better watch it. You aren't like us, and when my father finds out you're here, he'll make you into a slave and whip *you* unless you do what he tells you."

Maddie began to tremble. Mindy Lou continued to give her an intimidating look. "We'd better get back to bed before anyone finds out we left, or I'll tell everyone it was your idea." She raised her eyebrows and pointed to the whip.

They had just slinked into their cots when Miss Schill came into the room. "Young ladies, you're free to play under the big trees."

Maddie tried to avoid Mindy Lou as much as possible. Her thoughts turned again toward going back down the road. But, for now, she had to play along just a while longer. She sidled next to one of the younger girls. "What do you play?"

Charlotte, who also had big blue eyes like all the Henry cousins, answered, "Ring around the Rosy."

"That's a baby game."

Rebecca, whose blue eyes turned the same yellow-green that Mindy Lou's had, sneered. "Then what games do you play where you come from, Miss Maddie?"

"Well, mostly computer games".

"What's a computer?"

"It's this machine thing. An iPad. Everyone has them."

"What else do you do?"

"We watch television."

"What's that?" Cynthia asked.

Maddie felt so superior. Mindy Lou said she didn't know anything, but it was these girls who didn't know anything at all. "A television is like a picture, except you watch it and see people walk around and hear them talk."

The girls couldn't comprehend what she was telling them, so one of the cousins changed the subject. "Let's play with our dolls." Off they went to get them.

Maddie called after them. "Do you have Barbies?' but all she received was another blank look from each girl.

After a while, the music teacher, a jolly-looking man with a pink bald head and round body, arrived and called the girls inside for their lesson.

"Time to sing scales and motets," Cynthia said.

"What are motets?" Maddie asked.

"Really old songs," Cynthia answered.

"I know a really old song!" offered Maddie. She jumped up with air guitar in hand and belted out, "Rock around the Clock."

The girls laughed, but the music teacher couldn't have been more appalled. His face turned bright red, and he looked as if he would explode. He shrieked at Maddie, who felt certain he was going to hit her. "You should be ashamed of yourself. I have *never* heard such atrocious music in my life."

After music, it was time to eat again. Cold biscuits and honey with buttermilk made up the meal. Miss Schill announced it was time to practice penmanship. Mattie had no idea what she meant, but she liked dipping the funny pen into the ink and dribbling it all over the paper.

For bath time, everyone took turns in the huge pan in the kitchen. After that, Maddie lay in bed. Only one thing was on her mind. She wanted to leave. She didn't want the master to return. She didn't want to be turned into a slave. But it was so dark, she was afraid if she left now, she'd get lost. She decided to wake up early, before everyone else, and go home.

Maddie woke to the governess telling the girls to dress and eat quickly, because the schoolmaster was coming today. There was a classroom upstairs, and that's where the girls headed after their meal. The schoolmaster asked Miss Schill to stay and help him with the two extra students. Then he noticed Madison.

"I see we have another pupil," commented the man in the long black coat with bushy black eyebrows and ridiculous looking glasses on the end of his nose. "Let's see what you know. What's 10 times 16?"

"I don't know. We don't do multiplication until third grade."

"Very well. Find England on the globe."

Maddie recognized a globe, but no one had ever asked her to find something on it. She was smart and figured England started with an E, so she pointed to the first E word she saw, Egypt. The girls all laughed behind their hands.

"Hmm, so you don't know multiplication and you don't know geography. Here's an easy one. Who is the President of the United States of America?"

Of course, she knew the name of the President, but Maddie refused to answer. She didn't want the teacher to yell at her again.

Some of the cousins, whom Maddie realized liked her and didn't want her to fail again, whispered, "Mr. Buchanan."

"Answer my question!" The schoolmaster was not amused.

Still, Maddie refused to answer.

"She doesn't know," Mindy Lou hissed to Rebecca. "I knew she wasn't from here."

With a stony look, Maddie stared straight ahead. All the girls began to laugh in their high-pitched voices. To Maddie, they sounded like mad cats ready to pounce, biting and scratching at her. Out of the corner of her eye, she saw that the schoolmaster had taken a wooden paddle from a hook on the wall.

She started to get up to run, but Miss Schill grabbed her by the shoulders. The sweet, pretty lady's eyes turned wild, her expression threatening. "You will not be disrespectful to the schoolmaster. There's only one thing to do with such a naughty girl who is disrespectful to her elders and who makes up things like you've been telling the other girls."

As the governess clutched Maddie's arm and took her from the classroom, Mindy Lou had a smirk on her face. Maddie wondered if

Mindy Lou had been led away like this.

"*Please*, Miss Schill," Maddie pleaded as she thought to herself, *I have to get away from all these people with whips and paddles, who keep grabbing me.*

"Not another word!" The governess led the scared child downstairs and outside to something that looked like a slide at the playground but much wider. It was really a heavy wooden lid. Holding onto Maddie with one hand that dug into her flesh, Miss Schill pushed the hinged door until it fell over on the ground revealing a dark staircase. The stairs led to a door in the foundation of the house.

Guiding her down the stairs, Miss Schill told Maddie, "Master told me the other governesses always put naughty children in here." She opened the door and shoved Maddie into a small dark room that had an ugly smell of rotten potatoes and wet dirt. "You will stay down here in the root cellar until Master comes back."

Maddie begged in her loudest voice, but she heard Miss Schill slam the heavy lid closed. Maddie was terrified. The room was dark, and she was alone. As her eyes adjusted to the darkness, she began to see cloth bags all around. She peered into a bag of apples and grabbed one to eat. At least, she wouldn't starve to death before Mindy Lou's father came back.

She finished the apple and curled up in a corner on the dirt floor and began to cry. "I wished I'd never walked into that stupid picture." She wiped away tears with her hands, grimy from the dirt floor. She missed her family; they were probably worried. She wiped at her runny nose with her hands. "Even if I don't starve," she sobbed, "Master will make me a slave, and if I don't work hard, he'll whip me. I'm only a little girl."

Was this what life was like for some people in the past? She had never heard of buying people, of whipping them to make them work. They may have laughed at her for not knowing how to find certain countries on a globe or not knowing her times tables, but at least *she* knew that what they were doing was wrong. Nobody deserved to be treated the way the so-called master treated those poor slaves.

Except for her crying, it had been perfectly still in the dark cellar, but a sound caught Maddie's attention. It sounded like someone was throwing rocks at the door. She listened for a while. No, not rocks, but rain. The room grew colder, and Maddie tried to wrap herself up in a small empty bag. It didn't even cover her legs.

The sound of gnawing caught her attention. She sat perfectly still, hoping the noisy creature wouldn't find her, but it squeaked and ran across her bare legs. She screamed. "A rat! A rat is going to eat me!"

Two young boys, slaves, ran by, trying to find shelter from the rain. They heard Maddie's screams coming from the root cellar. "Oh, probably Miss Mindy Lou," she heard one of them comment. "She's always getting herself in trouble."

"And," said the other, "when we let her out, she gives us apples."

The two worked together and swung open the cellar door. They dashed down the stairs and opened the inner door. It wasn't Miss Mindy Lou. It was something with a face made from mud, wrapped in part of a gunnysack, and it was running up the stairs after them! They hollered and ran as fast as they could up the stairs and away, while Maddie ran in the opposite direction, back toward the road.

It rained harder, but Maddie didn't let that, or the road that quickly turned to mud, stop her. She'd seen what was at the end of the road. She wanted to get back to her own place with bathrooms, Barbies, television, iPads, good food, and nice teachers. As she slogged through the mud and saw her exit, she felt something wonderful in her heart. More than her modern comforts, Maddie appreciated the importance of living in a land where no one was a slave, and it didn't matter what you knew if you didn't know how to do the right thing.

She landed in a heap on the sofa. She was safe. She was home.

"There you are, Sweetie, it's time for lunch!" Grandma came in and stared at Maddie. "Why is your face so dirty, and where did you get that funny old dress?"

Before Maddie could answer, Grandma Henry raised her voice. "And your shoes. They're covered in mud. Get *off* the sofa right now!"

***

Perspective paintings have intrigued me from the time I took an art class in college. From then on I've sought out the "vanishing point" in such renderings and wonder what was hidden beyond that point. For my story AT THE END OF THE ROAD, I wanted to write a science fiction fantasy about imagining myself as a little girl who falls in love with a painting that features a road flanked by trees. One day she sets out to follow the road and winds up at another place in another time. As the story progressed, I realized it had become more political science than science fiction. With suggestions from the editor, I was able to transform it into a time travel piece featuring a child heroine.

Alice Marks

TURNING THE TIDE

What is it about these Navy guys, with their broad shoulders, gleaming chests, lean bodies, and long muscled arms? And their cigarettes?

With a smile, I regard the two framed vintage photos that bracket the computer monitor on my desk. On the right, Mike Finch, my late husband; on the left, Ernie Dangelo, my new love. Though the photos picture men in their early twenties, they were taken decades apart. My husband's photo is so old it's black and white, glossy, with a decorative trim. The newer photo is a Kodachrome, but time has adulterated the colors, making the yellows ochre, the reds dusty rose, and all the greens drab.

Yet there are more similarities than differences. Both men are short-haired and shirtless, those muscular arms resting on knobby knees clothed in fatigues, cigarettes dangling from hands caught for a moment in repose. Despite their rakish sailor smiles, the stress of war furrows their brows and clouds their gaze.

The two finest men I have known. Ah, my dear departed husband. Through a lifetime of service you survived many a battlefield only to die a senseless death, felled by a faceless enemy. Quite a few years older than I, he was bound to pass on before me, but not so soon. We were supposed to grow old together, spend our golden years enjoying the fruits of a lifetime of labor.

And my new love, brow permanently wrinkled, but not by the horrors witnessed during the Vietnam conflict, though they are as fresh today as they if they'd happened yesterday. No, you still reel from the pain of a fractured family.

Not fair. Not fair at all.

If I could, I would roll back time. Then Mike wouldn't have suffered and died a stupid, wasteful cancer death, and Ernie would once again live the family-man life that he loved.

Lifting my hands from the keyboard, I fold them in my lap and tilt back my desk chair. I think to myself, *I could do it. I could turn back time.* I'm a novelist. I invent entire universes, events, people so real that my characters have their own fan clubs. If I concentrate hard enough, I could connect with the Universe, put the thought out there with all of my being and with such intensity, that it would become reality. Mike would live a deservedly long life; he'd be robust, energetic. Ernie would find himself in his last home with his boys, even his former wife.

I shudder with a frisson of terror.

What if I am successful? Undoing the events that led to Mike's premature demise and Ernie's misfortunes could mean that I would never meet either of them. The very thought makes my eyes sting and squeezes my heart. Am I willing to pay that price for their happiness?

I glance again at their photos, the answer is clear.

I will need to immerse myself completely in my writer "zone" where I tune out the real world and tune in the sights, sounds, smells, and sensation of the one that I imagine. A beach walk usually helps me to clear my head.

***

At the water's edge, I watch the tide come in. That's how we speak of it, as the tide coming in. From where does it start? Does it start in the middle of the ocean somewhere and fan out?

A foamy line of surf reaches my toes, then retreats. Going out, it gathers strength and builds a tiny wave only to be consumed by the incoming tide.

Or maybe not. Maybe the ebb tide only slips under the approaching surge? What if the tide starts here, at the shore, the ebb flow gaining height and power as it moves out to sea? I focus on the water as it streams away from me. I push it out, imagining it swelling, rogue waves cresting, foaming, not inches from my feet but miles beyond, driving the surface water away from it. At the ocean's center, ebb flows from surrounding coastlines converge in one towering crescendo, a humongous spouting pillar of water, thrust toward the sky before it all collapses with a crash and spreads back out to shore. Though world-champion surfers double-dare each other to try it, no one ever has or at least hasn't lived to tell about it. Navigators mind their tide charts assiduously to keep their ships well clear of it. As foreboding as the Bermuda Triangle, this mid-ocean tide convergence has far-reaching effects that rival even the most powerful tsunami.

***

"Petty Officer Finch, lay below," says the captain. "Report to sick bay."

"I'm fine, Captain. I've been seasick before, and I know I can handle it. I can perform my duties."

"You can't complete a sentence that isn't interrupted by a cough. What you've got could be contagious, and I can't have you infecting anyone else. The Midway Islands aren't far from the Convergence. Massive rogue waves have been spotted, and we have to stay on this course. We're going to need every able-bodied man at his post. If the doc releases you for duty, fine. Otherwise, stay below."

"Lead, follow, or get out of the way?" Mike Finch replies, minding not to cough again in front of the captain.

He gives Mike an indulgent smile. "You got it. Now go get that cough checked out."

***

Mike dangles his legs over the edge of the table. He tells himself that it's the chill of the sick bay examination room that's given him goose bumps, not fear as he awaits the doctor's diagnosis.

The doctor studies his notes and frowns. "Any history of cancer in your family?"

"I don't think so, sir," Mike replies, but another wave of goose bumps sweeps across his back.

The doctor purses his lips and shakes his head. "I can't say what it is at the moment. Not until I get some test results. Could be bacterial, viral. An allergic reaction. Fungal."

Not cancer, Mike prays.

"We'll need additional tests when we make port. Meanwhile, do you smoke?"

"Do I smoke?" Mike echoes. "Who doesn't aboard this tub?" He started smoking in his teens but got serious about it after enlisting. Lighting up punctuated just about every pause from work, and smoking helped to relieve some of the monotony of being at sea.

The doctor scribbles on a small pad, tears off a slip of paper, and hands it to Mike. "My prescription: Stop smoking. Immediately. It's aggravating whatever it is that's causing your cough. You think you can comply?"

Mike pulls on his shirt and removes his package of cigarettes from the chest pocket. With a deep sigh, he hands them to the doctor. "Yessir."

"Good. And best stay in your bunk until we can determine if you're contagious."

"Yessir." Mike tries not to grumble. Just where he wants to spend the rest of their mission to stop the Korean menace: swinging in a hammock in a stuffy hold, seasick and coughing his throat raw.

***

Chief Warrant Officer Mike Finch opens another file folder, unclips the bundled pages, and drops the fastener into a glass dish at his elbow. Emblazoned with the Bureau of Naval Personnel emblem, ashtrays just like it decorate nearly every horizontal surface in the BUPERS offices. A nonsmoker since his cancer scare some years ago, Mike finds that his ashtray serves as a handy catch-all for paperclips and erasers.

He studies the file. *Hmm, this sailor has had all too easy a career. Time for him to find out what it really means to be in the Navy.* "Off to Diego Garcia," Mike says with a diabolical chuckle. A tiny tropical coral atoll in the middle of the Indian Ocean, Diego Garcia's strategic location makes it ideal for a naval support facility, but it's so remote that nearly all food and equipment has to be brought in, and even some of the waste has to be shipped off the island. Its proximity to the mid-ocean Convergence impedes access even further, making naval operations and even island life itself a test of nerves.

Mike studies the next file. *Now this sailor needs a break.* Ernie Dangelo has served multiple tours in Vietnam. Mike Finch admires the dedication, but the fellow hasn't been home in over a year. He has a wife, two little children. Dangelo's kids are growing up without their father. It's way past time the man saw his family. Mike chews on his lower lip. Surely there's a way he can get Ernie Dangelo stateside.

***

Ernie Dangelo jabs his cigarette into the ashtray and grips his coffee cup so hard that it threatens to crumble. It's the neck of the man Lisa had the affair with that he'd like to get his hands around, he realizes.

Across the kitchen table, his wife stares into her cup. Her murmured "I'm sorry, Ernie," can barely be heard over the sound of the kids playing in the next room. "You were gone so long. I never heard from you. I didn't even know if you were ever coming back." She looks up, her brown eyes open wide and shining with unshed tears. "Can you ever forget? Can you ever forgive me?"

She has a point, Ernie thinks.

A world away, Vietnam and the challenges of service had consumed him. Doing his patriotic duty, making the world safe for democracy. He had bought the whole package, but he was wrong to assume that his wife could carry on, maintain a home, and raise two little ones by herself with so little support from him. He swallows hard. "It hurts. I can't just pretend it didn't happen."

A tear breaks away and trails down her cheek. Ernie reaches across the table and takes her hand. "Forget? I don't know that I'll ever forget. But forgive? Babe, I love you. I love the kids. I want us to be together, to be a family. I'll leave the service if that's what it takes. If you'll still have me..."

His wife dips her head. When she looks up, she's smiling through her tears. She bolts from her chair and throws herself into Ernie's embrace.

***

What is it about these Navy guys, with their broad shoulders, gleaming chests, lean bodies, and long muscled arms?

I lean forward for a better view of a Veteran's Day video posted on Facebook. It includes a number of vintage photographs. Now,

58

there's a black-and-white of one handsome guy from the Korean War. I'll bet it was his first time away from home. Oh, and here's a shot of some Vietnam veterans, my contemporaries. It's in color, but the passage of time has corrupted all the shades.

They all look so young, yet so ardent and grave. They were probably just starting out. Did these men put in their four years and leave? Or, did they stay in and go on to have brilliant naval careers?

I wonder if I would have enjoyed being a Navy wife. Would I have relished living in different cities and foreign lands, or would I come to dread having to move a household every few years?

I'll never know.

The video ends. Anyway, it's time I got going. If I want to get in a beach walk today, I had better get out there before the high tide driven by the mid-ocean Convergence swamps the shore.

***

Turning the Tide began during a meeting of the Rockport (Texas) Writers Group. Once we've tackled operational matters such as upcoming events we're hosting or projects we'd like to sponsor we take on a writing exercise such as writing to a prompt. As a novelist, that's usually the only time that I write anything short.

On this particular occasion the challenge was to write something inspired by a photograph. I still have the handwritten draft of the opening scene and it was a time-travel story from the get-go, but I recall thinking then that it would be a longer work, a novella at the very least. I had other novel-length works in progress so *Turning the Tide* languished in a "story ideas" file.

Years later I happened to write another short story just on a whim. I shared it with the person who inspired it. He liked it so well that I offered it up for read-and-critique. The praise that I got for it boosted my confidence about writing short fiction. When Creative Alchemy announced it was accepting submissions of time travel stories, I saw the opportunity to take *Turning the Tide* out of limbo and develop it. I like it as a short story and feel no compulsion to make it a longer work.

Devorah Fox

STARING INTO

My first clue time travel could be possible was in the barber's chair the day before my girlfriend's funeral.

Andy lifted his pen and shaking hand from the paper. The clock on the stove read 10:06. *Why did I wait so long to write this?*

Because in less than two hours, he might cease to exist, if his plan even worked. How do you pack up for that? He'd call his dad on the way to work, but he had to be subtle. *Probably won't even answer.*

Andy crossed out 'my' and wrote 'our' between the lines before 'girlfriend,' but it was too sloppy. He tore the page out and gripped the pen harder. Holding his wrist to steady his strokes, he started his first line over. *My first clue... our girlfriend's funeral.*

She died coming to visit me at work. If I cease to be, and you get her, it will be for the best. I can't go on knowing I caused such a beautiful life to end. I have great joy offering myself for her life. I would do it a million times over.

Andy considered starting over again. He wasn't trying to make the future him or past him (however this ended) feel bad for him. If he failed, there would be enough time for that. *No, just keep going.*

Back to the first clue, Andy wrote. *Two days ago, my barber noticed a scar that couldn't have been there. A healed scar. Mandi didn't say anything because it isn't that big and is right under the hair line on my neck, but Jerry noticed. I looked at the camera footage at work—the one over my back making sure I only watch cameras at my desk—and I caught the scar appear at 11:58 PM, June 6th.*

Man, did my insides curl at that sight. I mean, I had been pretty freaked out by Jerry's comment, "Did you cut yourself since last time?"

There was no explanation. A minor surface scratch wouldn't leave the fat scar I had. Even if I had fallen and lost consciousness, there would have been a scab I would have noticed at least by the next time I washed my hair—let alone the blood that surely would have stained my clothes. I don't drink and don't have a history of seizures or losing consciousness (as you know, I hope), but also moot points considering I never noticed the wound. I didn't know what to expect watching the video—it's still hard to believe—but I had to do something.

Okay, so here's how I think timeline B went through time.

The facts are: He sat in one position watching the surveillance camera footage from 10:58 until 11:58. I watched from a side view angle camera to check if his eyes were open. They were. And didn't seem to move, though that was hard to tell.

That's it. The scar just appeared.

There's a high likelihood nothing will happen when I try. Or that I'll succeed. Staring at one place for an hour straight is the hardest thing I've ever tried, and I have a lot of doubts writing this because I am nowhere near reaching an hour.

He checked the clock. 10:21. *Crap.* He hadn't even changed yet.

I have a theory about tonight, he wrote. *About why timeline B did it before midnight. About why he appeared on the sixth. I think her birthday is the window. Like a second birthday. I don't know. Maybe it makes no sense. But I'd rather think of this being the miracle way than the alternatives I might end up in if this is a way to time travel.*

Welcome to our nightmare.

<u>*If I fail, please save her.*</u>

Andy folded the note. *What if I travel to a timeline where he doesn't know her and I put in his mind to go find her and somehow that kills her?*

He shook his head and put the note in his pocket. Thoughts like those were not helpful. He didn't want them in his last few hours alive.

He sat in the driver's seat of his Buick Skyhawk, a bag of last night's McDonald's smelling his car up with ketchup and old grease. He took his phone out and found his dad's number. 10:35. He was going to be late. He started the car and hesitated to press 'call.' What in the world would he say? What if they fought about his lack of money? Budget chat with Dad was the last thing he wanted in his last ninety minutes. Andy thought of the good times, when his dad had been home to play catch. Though mostly he wasn't. How his dad… warm memories failed to come to mind, only awkward, tough times where his dad was too preoccupied with getting them back on track financially, with not getting kicked out of their house, with the latest car repair need.

10:37. *Oh man.* Andy pressed the call button. He switched it to speaker phone and backed into an oil stained parking spot behind his apartment building. The line rang as he pulled around the tan brick home he may never see again—no big problem there—and turned onto College Ave.

"Hi, Andrew." His dad sounded surprisingly pleased, as though none of the bad memories that had come to mind ever happened. It was the 4th of July weekend, and he was excited for his son to come home and grill some hot dogs. They'd wear matching Cubs hats and talk about how Lester was pitching this year.

Andy needed that to be real, even for a few minutes. "I love you, Dad."

His dad coughed or something on the other line. "What's wrong? Are you in danger?"

Tears burned through his eyelids. He wanted so badly to tell him the truth, to have him save him and somehow fix everything without needing to sacrifice himself.

"Andrew." His voice grew multiples more urgent.

Andy realized what his only recourse could be to keep his dad from ruining his plans. "What?" he asked, pulling out the aggression he'd grown used to while speaking to his father.

"What's going on? Are you in trouble?"

"No. I'm fine." He kept up the attitude. For once in his life, the tone was accompanied by eternal love. "I just wanted to tell you that. See if it made me happy, like a movie I just saw."

"Sure. I love you, too, Son." He sniffed. "Are you sure there's nothing wrong?" His voice choked out. He sounded like a pansy.

Andy swallowed so he didn't sound the same. He struggled to control his breathing. His grip on the steering wheel staggered, but he kept the car between the lines. A truck with a wooden bed holding lawn mowers sped past on the other side.

"I'm sure, Dad. I do love you. Tell Sarah I said I love her, too. I'm heading onto the freeway. I need to let you go."

"Where are you going?"

"Work. I gotta go, Dad."

"Okay. I love you, too, Son."

"Bye," Andy whispered and hung up the phone. He wiped his eyes. His father's words coated him in an aloe of hope while his skin burned with confusion and fear. The freeway had only one car in the far lane when he sped to pace with traffic. Holding his phone, he thought of whom else he could call. Even if he knew how to reach his birth mother, he wouldn't call her. She had abandoned him long ago.

He thought of Mandi's funeral. Her mother hadn't lifted her head or stopped crying; her weak and staggered steps guided by her sobbing husband to the outburst at the pastor's scripture quote of, "then face to face." Andy's soul shriveled in that moment of open rebuke, indirect, but in his heart it pointed squarely at him. He'd taken her from them. A mother who deserved to see her daughter grow old.

He made it to the light at the top of the off ramp at 10:52, nervous he'd miss the 10:58 mark. Really, he was about to throw her life away a second time because he still wasn't mature enough to get anywhere early. He drove through the red light, sped over the bridge and up the hill to the entrance of the Quest building.

Andy sprinted through the grass toward the front door. Carl watched through the window pane, hefting his book bag onto his shoulder. Andy swiped his ID card at the first set of doors and entered that week's five-digit pin. A red light and angry chime responded. *Crap.* 6-2-3-7-6 he thought as he forced his fingers to hit the right keys, ignoring the need to glance at his watch. Green. *Click.*

"What's the rush, Andy?" Carl always spoke to him like he was ten pay grades above. *You're just a security guard like me.*

"Don't worry about it." Andy squeezed past and sat in the chair, hiking it up to where he normally sat. Everything had to be the same. The time was 10:57. Andy exhaled, blinked. Then stared straight into the middle camera. The west atrium view of a garbage can set beside the double glass door exit.

"See you later, weirdo."

Andy kept his stare on the garbage can through an awkward silence that Carl let drag.

Carl finally turned and walked out the front. "Freakin' psycho." The words hurt in a time desperate for confidence, but he forced them back. He wasn't going to let Mandi go because of that loser.

The west atrium showed an elevator on the right and the concrete outside lit by the exterior flood lights, a view as familiar as his face in the mirror. A small creature, probably a chipmunk, scurried into the picture. Andy fought the curious urge to look as it cut into the grass past the walkway.

His eyes strained against the bored need to look around. Ever since he'd come up with this theory about the power of focus, a kind of open-eyed meditation that could harness the body's energy, he had practiced staring at things and timing how long before a blink or moment of weakness sent his focus off target. Thirty-four minutes and twenty-seven seconds was the longest he'd gone. For nearly two weeks he had read articles on meditation and watched YouTube videos of Chi experiments. One had a guy who created fire just by focusing and sending his shaking body's attention through his hand.

The problem with that was Andy B didn't shake. He was cool as a cucumber. The video had shown Carl, without sound, always seeming to try and pester Andy B, but Andy B calmly sat, posture perfect and stared at his monitor. For the ten days prior to the 6th, when Andy B became Andy A, he was almost always in that position.

How long had he been practicing? Was he trying to save Mandi, too? If so, he failed.

I can't fail.

Andy A's eyes had grown stronger with practice, but there was no avoiding the pull to observe something, anything else. Tiny puppeteers tugged on the tendons behind the eyeballs. Long, slow steps backward increased the strain.

He'd asked one of the other guards, Martin, an Afghan vet, how he had survived eight hour shifts sitting at his turret, watching and waiting for a threat to surface. Martin had said the trick was learning not to check the time.

That helped motivate Andy against the temptation to see the clock. He pretended he was a soldier, and failure would cost lives. Technically, it did. At least one. *But so will success…*

He passed the time wondering how much of him would continue on, if it would be like dying at all. He considered his past and what made him worthy of such a blessing, to be given the gift of life and love when it was his fault they'd been taken away.

He'd thought about his sports past, how he was one day late asking the baseball coach if tryouts were still open. He'd proven his talent in city ball, if he'd not been a day late, he might have built up his skill playing for his school, earned a baseball scholarship…There was no second chance there. His life could have been different if he'd taken other roads moments before the two car accidents he'd had afterwards, which totaled his cars and cost him not only thousands of dollars, but jobs, summers without baseball, and a back that he'd grown used to having chronic pain. Like the emotional losses he couldn't get back, his back pain reminded him daily how certain curses can be eternal.

The L5 area in his spine ached as his weight pressed on his tailbone, even in the posture-correct position he'd also seen Andy B use. He hadn't practiced that part, or anticipated how the stress might make it worse. *How did he do this?*

He didn't need a clock to know he was miles from 11:58. His back was already aflame.

Meditation techniques often spoke of being in the present, of not worrying about the past, but that was even more boring than his normal job. And the present pain was quite unbearable, thank you very much.

Plus, if these are my last thoughts, I don't want to waste them on nothing...

The more Andy thought about his past and how small, seemingly insignificant decisions or actions could have improved his life, the more angry he became at God or chance about who and where he was.

And why am I the one who discovers time travel? Or whatever this is...God really screwed up on that call.

Maybe he wasn't the only one. The randomly changing entrance code seemed a bit like overkill. Mr. Sibowitz was an anal boss, and maybe that was why. What if he was the reason Andy B failed? Did he give him the scar? Was he watching Andy right now?

A bird soared into the grey light outside the west atrium. *No.* He kept his eyes on the garbage can. *Trash. Trash. Trash...*he thought until he'd fallen into a zone again. What was he thinking about?

Oh yeah. What if others discovered time travel this way? The bored ones more motivated to cross into the strange corner the populous tried to keep hidden with their distractions and relationships. Who needs relationships when you can stare at a garbage can for an hour without blinking? This is paradise!

The mention of blinking awakened the itch digging into his eyes. The irritation had been the source of half his failures. The worst part about the itch was it started within half an hour. It was like running a marathon (he imagined) only to find at the end it was only the halfway mark, the rest would be run barefoot over hills of exposed shards and hot coals.

This is the night. There is no retreating from this chance. Love and life are on the other side. Believe that.

Dry flame cracked his eyeballs. *Think of something else, you're not there yet.*

He imagined Mr. Sibowitz's tracking sensors in his chair. Waiting for him to get to the edge, and then snatch the power for himself while leaving Andy to a life of failure and misery.

No. That's not truth. That's imagination. It has to be.

He thought back to Mandi. Then like an accidental channel switch, his mind flicked to girls unlike Mandi, ones he wished to forget, but would be forced to remember. Like the blind date who'd turned from their awkward driveway meeting to a phone inside to call for rescue. The girl he made out with at the baseball field and then felt beetle ridden with guilt because he didn't like her as much as she liked him. He'd just wanted someone there, even after he knew she wasn't enough. Soon after, he'd gone to parties. He'd walk through the crowded, strange homes with stairs that led up to off-limits rooms, basements with pool tables or old couches full to capacity by people who stared without smiles. Faces eager for him to turn around so they could forget his awkwardness. Looks that said coming there was uncool and he should have known better. He had become like the girl who falls in love with the wrong guy.

And now he stared at a garbage can. Mandi would appreciate him if she were here. Appreciate the sores opening up under the volcanic cracks carving through his eyeballs.

The dirty metal rim and untucked black bag glared at him. Look at your desperate need for approval, it said. At your desperate ploy to change the world. Change yourself if you want to make a change. Accept where you are and move forward. You're not a ship casting its way through the waves. You're not even the garbage that floats with the current. You're the rock some kid throws that doesn't skip. You move by the power of someone else. You pass by, and when you impact with the force we survive on, you sink.

So why don't you just sink, man?

Because I'm not a rock.

What makes you think you can lie to me? I'm in your head. I know who you are. You're a rock. As ugly and uninteresting as I've ever seen. Sinking to the ocean bottom where the current will erode you into nothing. Can a rock do anything to stop the ocean? Can a rock swim? Develop gills to breathe? No. There is no life, nor power, nor impact in your future. You were made to fade.

Maybe. Maybe so, before Mandi. But after…After, meeting her I began to evolve. I made her laugh, smile, feel loved—even if I didn't tell her. I would now if given the choice. I've seen my weakness, and I refuse it. I have a chance now to break the curse, and I will embrace it.

That was just your moment in the air. Tricking you to think there is a way to change who you are. You're still a rock. You'll hit the water like everyone else. Then all that's left is to sink, to stop, to turn into dust and then disappear.

Upside down mountains bore into the jelly of his eyes, demanding he shut them to end the pain.

It's not time. I've been here before and let your reality win.

He sensed footsteps in the cover of silent distance. Mr. Sibowitz coming for his undeserved prize.

Tonight is different. Tonight I climb. The mountain's peaks cut me. I bleed, but do not cease. I may be the rock, but my airborne course will carry on.

The garbage became just garbage, silently shaming him for his conversation with inanimate metal. The polished rock turned into a catcher of waste.

A door clicked open behind him.

No, this is my prize.

A cool breeze swept through his eyes and embraced his soul, letting them shut.

No!

He peeled back his eyelids and flicked his attention at the clock. 11:58.

Why was he so afraid? He looked over his shoulder at a closed door and dark hall beyond. Was someone there?

Mandi should be here any minute. He smiled and stood. Back pain mixed with foggy confusion, as though he'd just woken from a year-long nap. He walked to the door, unable to stop blinking, and unsure why his eyes itched so.

Joy carried him outside like a white bird with ten-foot wings.

From the street, Mandi's burgundy Honda pulled into the incline drive. Her headlights shrouded her as she left the glow of the floodlight near the entrance and ascended the drive. Andy pushed the second door open to the warm summer night. Anticipation shivered through him as though walking toward something too great to be real. Yeah, it was Mandi's birthday, and of course he was glad to see her, but why was he tearing up?

Mandi parked and turned to watch him as she unbuckled her seatbelt, lifting a smile he thought he'd never enjoy again.

Why?

He let go and accepted the embarrassment of tears. She threw her door shut and ran with a bashful grin. His favorite. He deserved to cry with joy at the sight of her.

"Did I make it?" she asked as she entered his airspace, gifting him with the scent of her wildberry spray. She slowed, staring into his eyes. "Are you crying?" Confusion turned to respect.

Andy looked away and wiped his sleeve across his face, trying to hide the action by also taking his phone out of his crowded pocket. A folded paper and his keys blocked its easy path.

"What's wrong?" She lifted his chin to face her.

Face to face. Why did those words speak of memory?

What could be wrong? He smiled in never feeling more right. "Nothing. I guess I'm just happy to see you." He woke his phone. 12:00. "Midnight. July 6th. Happy 21st, Mandi."

"Thanks." She considered him for a moment. He moved in to hug her. She accepted, pulled back, and kissed him. In an ocean of time, that moment could float forever.

But even as it ended, her up-close eyes sparkled with more to come. "Did you get me anything?"

Andy panicked. He didn't. A perfect opportunity missed because what? He'd forgotten? He knew it was her birthday, and yet it was the farthest thing from his mind. He had invited her to meet at midnight. He *must* have, even if he didn't remember. Neither did he remember what he'd planned to do when she arrived.

The strange paper in his pocket. He took it out.

She snatched it before he could unfold it. "What's this?" She spread it open and her glee floundered. She turned the paper to gain the glow from the floodlights on the building behind them. Andy leaned in to see what it said. It appeared to be blank.

She turned, her eyebrows bent low. "Okay? I don't get it."

He didn't either. But he had to say something. This was her birthday, and he really liked her. Newness like a generous second chance filled him with hope. "Before you, my life was full of scratched out words and stories I've longed to forget." *Okay* ... She wasn't sure where he was going. He wasn't either, but a strong sense urged him that being sure wasn't what mattered. It was that he continued to move forward. "But the joy you give me is like a blank page. I don't care about the past, because I'm too excited for the future."

Her stare tasted his joy and embraced it for more. He had plenty to spare. "I'm excited, too."

"Good." He took her hands.

"Thank you. I'm really glad you're in my life, too."

The answer had come to a question beyond his grasp. The question of lost memories and how he'd arrived in this place of life and time. Whatever it was, he knew the answer was good. It was right before his eyes.

***

I like to take circumstances I'm dealing with and insert them into the character aspect of my stories. In "Staring Into," I thought, what the heck is the point of my life sitting here at this job staring at monitors?

The biggest challenge I have is enduring boredom. I thought, what if a security guard reached such an elevated level of focused boredom--where he stared at one spot on the monitor for so long-- that he was able to travel in time. After I had that idea, I had to find a way to connect to his heart and why traveling in time would be exciting and affect his heart.

Timothy C. Ward

THE GHOST OF TIME

Agent Fogarty slipped through the halls, trying hard to keep her focus through the stinging array of fluorescent lights and her fading consciousness. The wound at her side pulsed, blood soaking her hand and uniform. With her non-gun hand, she kept her finger over the trigger and searched each hall for signs of her target.

She had been through worse scrapes before. She could do this. The problem was with her target, who seemed to continually be two steps ahead of her at all times. If she didn't get to him and stop him from negatively impacting the future she was from, she would have no home to return to. She would likely be forced to stay in an era she didn't belong in, or worse, she would inadvertently create a paradox. Who knew what that would do?

A sound echoed from the corridor in front of her.

Agent Fogarty leaned her back against the hall adjacent to the opening. She stared at the stone grey trim stacked against off-white walls and polished stone floors. Taking a few deep breaths, she steadied her shoulders and steeled her nerves. With a shove from the wall, using more of her waning strength, she pushed herself forward, stumbling toward the other wall then leaning against it for support. More pain gnawed at her side. She had minutes left to catch the target before she fell unconscious.

Once the surge of pain passed, she peeked down the corridor, where the noise came from. Ebony curls fell into her face. She blew them away to get a better glance. Only dark shadows and a pallid hall took up her vision.

If only he hadn't gotten that lucky shot off, she would've likely had him in custody and in transport back to the proper time. Her time. Not some sick, half-deserted hospital floor in the middle of downtown Houston 1986. When she rounded the corner, she longed for her Los Angeles home waiting 450 years in the future. She longed for the fresh, pollution-free air, the automatic cars programmed to drive themselves, including memorizing the addresses of her most visited locations. For January Fogarty, she missed her cat Galaxy the most.

Sure, she had family, but family only went so far when living alone and having no one to cuddle with late at night. Of course, had she not caught her fiancé in bed with that. . .

Agent Fogarty shook her head to clear her mind. She couldn't allow herself to revisit portions of her life, even negative memories that would normally give her just the right *oomph* to carry out a mission. Truth be told, she began feeling like it was the end. But she couldn't allow it to be the end. It *wouldn't* be the end.

Not if I can help it, it won't.

She stumbled across the hall and approached a deserted desk. A door behind that most likely led to an office where files were kept. The door off to the side of a small waiting room appeared as though it would lead much farther.

She inched closer, leaning against the door only to have it give way too easily and slam against the wall, recreating the sound she heard from before. She nearly tumbled to the floor but managed to catch herself on the other door. It held a paper sign taped to the center, instructing caution when opening the door, as it was susceptible to slamming.

Lucky for her, the target didn't stop to read the sign before he charged through. Unlucky for her, she did the same damn thing, most likely alerting him of her proximity. Either he was hiding and was aware of how close she was, or he discovered how close he was to getting away. Maybe both.

Either way, she stepped through the narrow passage toward a series of offices and cubicles. If her target hid somewhere within the room, instead of moving farther out and getting away, it would be nearly impossible to catch him. The only hope she had was her night specks, but the target ensured those were knocked off when they got into their altercation. January adjusted her jaw again from the right hook he laid into her with. It ached, and there was a slight grinding sound when she moved her jaw a certain way.

That can't be good.

She decided to put her concern off until she made it home. *If* she made it home. Time travel was tricky, and she had to be careful of how she did things. One small ripple in the time line could cause all sorts of disarray in the future. That's why only a select few were allowed to become Time Ghosts.

A wave of dizziness rotated through her, forcing her to stop in her steps. She closed her eyes and waited for the moment to pass. Her legs gave out from under her, sending the Time Ghost to the floor, and this time, she barely felt a twinge of pain.

Oh no . . .

"It's not what you think!" the target said as he approached.

So you keep insisting. The question is why?

He was a different one, that much was certain. Usually, targets offered longwinded explanations for committing their crime. They never denied it. In fact, none of her targets to this point had much room to deny their crimes. The proof was in their jump. Kind of hard to fight that evidence.

She tried to glimpse her target hidden in the shadows, she didn't even have the strength to hold up her weapon anymore.

"So you keep . . . telling me." Her words came out slurred and half-spoken.

"Please, let me help you, and I promise to explain everything."

There was movement to her left. Someone--or something--slowly crept closer to her and seemed too low to the ground. She blinked a few times but couldn't get a clear image. Part of her understood what to do, and the other part didn't have the strength to flinch, much less lift her weapon.

She took a few breaths and tried to mutter something about not coming any closer or she'd shoot. Had she been coherent, she would've asked why he wanted to help her when he was the one who shot her. Be that as it may, her eyes grew heavy as unconsciousness won over.

She gave into the darkness.

***

When January opened her eyes, it took her a moment to realize she wasn't dead, at home, or back in her own time. She was somewhere else entirely. She expected to feel more pain than she did, but the aching had dulled. As she took in the short stretch of her body, she discovered her suit was missing. She wore an itchy fabric blend that was warm and soft at the same time. A loose tank covered her top half. Both of them were a dark, steel grey. She shifted her toes, the way she did when she'd first wake up. They too, were covered in something thick and warm, though they were smooth and soft.

"Sleeping Beauty awakes!" A man to her side spoke, causing her to snap her attention to him. He was stout and wore an obnoxious colorful shirt with leaves and giant tropical flowers. His grey hair was cut in the way that the back was longer than the top. He wore thick, plastic frame glasses on his nose, and he plundered away on a massive collection of boxes with enough cords to strangle half an army.

Ugh, eighties technology. So retro and always over the top.

She held up both of her hands to inspect each and ensure all her fingers were still covered in smooth, chestnut-toned velvet. All of her gear had been removed.

"My name is not Sleeping Beauty." She dropped her hands to her sides. "It's January Fogarty."

She turned her attention to the gentleman in time to see his eyebrows rise in rounded arches. "Well, that's quite an unusual name, January Fogarty. I'm Phoenix."

"Phoenix?"

He nodded, a bit of sweat shaking from his hair. "Yup, Phoenix."

She tried to sit up with as little pain as possible. Only a minor tug filled her side, which caused her to pause, eyebrows pinching together in confusion. She lifted up the side of her shirt and pulled away the gauze just enough to inspect her wound. She gasped at the graph that was done.

"Impossible," she whispered.

"Nope. Not impossible. Not when your savior has the technology from the time you came from."

She lifted her gaze to Phoenix. "You know about me? About what I am?"

He smiled, letting a short chuckle filter between his lips. "Yup! I know a lot of stuff. Like how to make coffee!"

He held up a bright yellow ceramic cup of primo bean juice. Distrust tugged at her insides; who was this man? And did he work for or with her target? She supposed if he wanted to kill her, his choice of weapon certainly wouldn't have been coffee. January mustered a slight smile in response and gave a nod. Phoenix bounced around his horseshoe shaped contraption of gizmos and gadgets, lighter on his feet than seemed possible for a man of his girth. As he approached, he did a little dance and a spin, ending with the cup out toward January.

"You have such beautiful eyes. Almost like a forest at dawn."

January tried to sip her brew without choking. The bitter liquid had cooled considerably but was still enjoyable. The flavor danced along her taste buds. "Thank you . . . for the coffee, and the compliment. I think."

He nodded, parking his rear on the square table in front of the sofa.

"So," he smacked his lips, "tell me about your mission."

She peered at him from over the rim of her coffee cup, a small crease appearing right above the bridge of her nose. "If you know as much as you say you do, then you know I cannot tell you anything."

He nodded with a sigh and a smack of his knee. He stood and returned to his collection. "You'll come around. But I'll tell you this, everything is not what it seems. They do not know what they're talking about. Well, they do, but you wouldn't believe me. Not yet, anyway."

January stood from her bed and stretched her arms above her head, arching her back and feeling her stretch deep within her core. She let out a soft sigh. "You're right. I probably wouldn't believe you. Where is my target? More importantly, how did I get here?"

"All understandable questions," Phoenix said.

"And I may have some of your answers."

The target stood just five feet from her, unarmed and nearly unclothed. Umber toned muscles rippled along shoulders, arms, chest, and abs. He wore a pair of sweat pants matching the ones January wore. She lowered her gaze to the clothes she wore, and their considerable bagginess.

Within an instant, she snapped her gaze back to her target. "You almost killed me!"

"The shot was a mistake. I wasn't aiming for you. Believe me, I'm a better shot than that."

To further prove his point, he turned his tight, thick back toward her to show off the glistening brand of the United Union of Time Protectors inked onto his skin, right between his shoulder blades. It was the same all Ghosts received the moment they graduated from the academy.

The transmutation circle on his back consisted of one large ring, bordered by another. From a single point at perfect center, surrounded by a band with an alchemical symbol, twelve lines shot out, stretching beyond the original rings, boundless by time. At each of the twelve points rested another circle holding one of twelve alchemical symbols. Though the order of the first twelve could be different from Ghost to Ghost, the center one always remained the same: the breath of life. Within the initial bordering rings are the runic commands of time travel. And finally, the twelve lines representing the twelve hours of a clock are wrapped by ribbons of runes meant to offer protection, safe travel, stealth, and other abilities pertaining to successful missions for the agent.

January gaped at the man's backside until he glanced over his shoulder and caught her mouth hanging open. He turned around, breaking her gaze of his backside and knocking her from her disbelief.

"How?"

He smiled. "It's a very long story. One you definitely need to hear."

She shook her head again. "No. Turn back around."

He hesitated for a moment before nodding and obliging her request. January didn't waste a second. She approached him and lifted her long, slender fingers to the slightly raised transmutation circle on his back. She carefully gauged every line and rune with her fingertips, focusing on each minute detail. She could tell the difference between one recently given, and one that's been used a few times. This man wasn't only a Ghost, he was a veteran. But he didn't appear much older than her.

January took a few steps back, letting her hand fall to her side. A pinch formed in the center of her forehead as her lips pulled into a taught frown. He turned around slowly to face her, the agent sent to kill him, wearing little more than a calm expression on his face.

Phoenix stood by, arms crossed over his shoulders, watching their stare down with fascination. The tension climbed, setting sparks to light in tiny bursts throughout the room. January took a breath, realizing it had been caused by her holding it in, trying to work through the puzzle she faced. If he's a Ghost, why was she sent on a mission to kill him?

"Were you about to kill the great-grandmother of Ferguson Delany?" January asked.

"No."

"Why are you in this time period?" She narrowed her eyes at him, carefully taking in every action.

"The same reason you were sent here."

She crossed her arms over her chest. "That doesn't make sense."

"It does if you think about it closely." He nodded his head toward her, as if the motion alone was supposed to make his point clearer.

January shook her head. "This isn't possible."

Panic rose within her, and he lifted his hands toward her, waving them up and down as he gently spoke to her. "I know this is a lot to take in. You are still under stress from the wound and losing so much blood. Please, sit. We can talk this over once you have had a chance to fully recover."

She sighed and stepped to the couch she had been on. She took a seat a little too hard, wincing at the pull on her side.

"Careful," Phoenix said, turning to one of his many monitors. "You don't want to pull your wound open. It was a bitch to seal it after Chuckles, here, got you to safety."

The room started to spin. Her stomach clenched. With a groan, she leaned over her knees, propping her elbows on them and taking deep breaths.

"My name is Carson, by the way. I'm not sure what headquarters told you or what they put to my identity, but I assure you, you are safe here." His voice moved closer to her.

"Where is *here*?" she asked, taking in deep breaths and slowly letting them out.

"An abandoned research facility in Houston."

She looked through her long, onyx lashes at the room around her. "An abandoned research facility, huh? Are you sure we're safe?"

"We're as safe as we can be."

"Does this facility have showers and working toilets?"

"The building was abandoned due to its troubled history. No one has had a heart or mind to tear it down. Teens come to party here every once in a while. It takes me or Phoenix to run them off, but for the most part, we're left alone. No one knows we're here. That, and the protection symbols we put up to ward against anyone actively searching for us." He sat next to her.

"There was a reason I asked about the toilets."

Carson stiffened. "Oh. Uh, follow me."

Without waiting for her to respond, he took off across the room and toward the hall he had stepped out of. January followed suit, noting the room they were in. It appeared more like a waiting room than anything, which didn't say research facility to her.

She followed Carson through darkened corridors. The man moved with military speed and precision.

No wonder you were hard to catch.

Strange, how none of that was covered in the briefing. She was sure the mission was legit. Somehow, she'd have to find a way out of the building, and then to a place where she could go back home to her own time.

"I want you to know you can come to me with any questions at any time," Carson said as he moved.

"If you're so protected here, why did you leave?"

He gazed over his shoulder, doing a double-take, and said, "Well, we have to go out looking for others like us. Give them a safe place to go. Plus, we do need food and supplies. And I work here. In this time, I mean."

"You're not supposed to do that!"

He shrugged. "I'm trapped here. Same as you. No one will be able to go back without being killed on sight. Your best bet is to remain here until you are healed, then we will reintegrate you into society, or you can stay with us. I can get you a job where I work. It's different from the whole time warrior thing, but it's enjoyable and less dangerous."

She let out an incredulous chuckle. "No thank you."

He stopped at a door then faced January. "Suit yourself. The offer still stands. This is your stop."

She stared cold at him for several long moments. "You're not going to stay out here, are you?"

"You're kidding me?"

She shook her head and flipped her hands out from her side.

"You're afraid of a man hearing you tinkle, fluff, or poo?"

She lifted her eyebrows in rounded arches and said, with as much venom as she could muster, "*Don't* talk to me like that again. I can break your leg in a fraction of a second. I'm a private person. I don't trust easily, and I have no reason to trust you, yet."

"I saved your life."

"To what end?"

Carson pressed his lips together and huffed a sigh. "Fine. Go. Just come straight back."

The fact he avoided her question didn't escape her notice. It was added to the bottom of a growing list of suspicions and things that weren't adding up. As Carson stepped around her and headed back toward the room they came from, she rotated, following his shrinking form until he was out of sight. She rushed into the bathroom, did her business, and checked her body for any marks or blemishes that shouldn't be there. Afterward, she poked her head through the doorway of the restroom. Peering down each side of the hallway, she decided to make a break for it while the getting was good.

***

Judging by the half destroyed signs on the walls and those hanging from the ceilings, Agent Fogarty was a few turns away from freedom. She had no idea what she was going to do once she was out of the building, but it didn't matter. Anything January Fogarty, Time Ghost, put her mind to, she was capable of doing. She smirked.

She turned the last corner, stopping short of running into Carson.

"What's out there, isn't for you. You'll find freedom, for a while. But in a few days or months or years, you will become a target of another Ghost. You may be able to outrun them, and you may not. You won't know what time they will come from. You won't know the technology they will bring."

"You knew I was coming, and you managed to shoot me and rescue me. I'm not really in the mood to listen to you." She tried to side-step around Carson, but he grabbed her arm, forcing her to face him.

"Think about this before you do something that could result in you losing your life."

"Let go of me," she said, yanking her arm free of Carson's grip.

"Just think. Try to remember everything you did before you did the jump."

"Whatever," she muttered as she continued through the hall, leaving Carson behind in his stewing.

"I may not be there to save you next time."

There won't be a next time.

She made the last turn and let the sight of the glass doors leading to her freedom soak in. A smile pulled on the edges of her lips, not quite making it all the way to her eyes. Her eyebrows, in fact, were pulling together, despite her stubbornness. Why couldn't she remember the very last thing she did before she made the jump?

What happened to me?

The normal routine of pre-jump check and her briefing was so second nature, she never once thought twice about the fact that everything she knew about her target was just there. She did have a rough landing, which knocked her out, but amnesia didn't work like that, and if it did, she would've remembered everything right as she stood several yards from the exit of the research facility she was taken to.

January rubbed her thumb and left forefinger together as she tried to think things through. She tried to make connections fit. The last thing she remembered was her friend and co-worker, Michelle, staring at the large projection of Carson rotating in a 360-degree view.

"He's cute," her friend said, taking in January's reaction.

January had stood with her arms crossed over her chest, brows knitting themselves together and her finger and thumb rubbing against each other in circles. She could never understand why her friend always wanted to set her up with all the wrong men. It was too soon for her to think about dating again anyway. January bobbed her shoulder. "If you say so. He's a criminal. He went rogue. I have to dispatch him."

She sighed. Auburn curls glided around her shoulders in soft waves. "Such a shame."

January laughed quietly. "You are horrible."

Her friend's reaction was to throw her hands in the air and turn toward her console . . .

How puzzling for January not to link a memory directly before or after that. She bit her lip, unwilling to buy the evidence that suggested what Carson and Phoenix said was the truth. It couldn't possibly be. Yet, she stood in the foyer of some facility in a year that didn't belong to her.

Steps crunched behind her.

Another deep breath, in and out.

Her fingers stilled as she turned around to face the man that puzzled her even more. His deep, dark eyes enveloped her with concern and a glance that she regarded as a shield, a front of self-perseverance. He leaned against the corner of the hall she had emerged from. His arms folded in front of him, bulging muscles rippling along each bend and curve, and one leg slightly bent while the other remained straight.

"You can't, can you?"

January cocked her head to the side, eyebrows pulled together taught.

"Remember," he said.

Another sigh left her lips as her shoulders deflated. "It's not possible."

Her words came out soft, almost in a whisper, but still traveled well enough for Carson to understand. He nodded and removed himself from the corner. "We can help you."

Carson held out his hand toward January, forcing her heart to drum harder. She had nowhere else to go, and with everything supporting him, she wasn't sure she could risk stepping out of the building just yet. Especially if there was already an assassin after her.

Taking Carson's hand, one thought processed through her mind . . .

What did I do that forced me to be condemned like this? Better yet, did my father know, and if he did, was he involved?

Carson started to lead January back through the halls. He kept glancing at her as they moved. Her lips were pulled down into a frown, and a crease settled itself between her eyebrows.

"You remembered something, didn't you?"

January sighed, long and heavy. "I did."

"If it makes you feel any better, when I got stuck here, I had no idea where I was or why. I thought it was a mistake. Nothing added up. Shortly after, I found Phoenix. He helped me to remember and figure out a way to live relatively under the radar in this time. We understood it would be a matter of time before someone else came.

We have the answers, I promise to share them. First things first, though. You need to eat and get rest. Of course, I'll be happy to help you uncover anything you need me to."

"You're a little too eager for me to trust you just yet." But, he did have answers she wanted. She wouldn't deny that.

"On the contrary. I'm eager because I've been there. I'm there still."

"Why did they send you here?"

Carson sighed heavily. "I learned too much, uncovered a few things I shouldn't have, and I got caught."

January mulled over Carson's words as he led her through the remaining maze of halls to the large room where Phoenix still sat at his collection of monitors and cables. He peered over his shoulder at the two as they entered, peering over the rim of his glasses with a gleam in his eyes.

"Welcome back, madam."

January smiled, despite the troubling thoughts rolling through her mind. "Thank you, Phoenix."

"Sure thing. You go ahead and lie down and . . . Hang on a second."

"What's going on?" Carson asked.

January furrowed her brow as a high pitched beeping started erupting from somewhere within the collection of retro-technology. She inched her way closer.

"Picking up some residual traces of energy. Too much for it to not be another jumper."

January pursed her brow. "What do you mean? Is this how you knew I was coming?"

Phoenix shrugged with a cock of his head and shoulder. "This is how we knew you were coming. Just not where you were coming from. It's likely that this burst is minutes old, and the ghost will be long gone by the time we return there."

"That was quick for someone to come through already," Carson said.

"How long does it usually take?" January asked.

He shrugged. "It's time travel. Who knows when they were sent from? Still, it's generally a bad idea to have two jumps in too close of a time period because of paradoxes."

January shook her head and rolled her eyes. "Of course. That's why they never send more than one Ghost."

"Precisely," Carson said. "Take yours for example. I've been here for six months before you came after me."

January leveled her eyes on Carson. "But you jumped . . . That doesn't make any sense."

"What?" he asked.

"Your jump supposedly happened hours before mine. Literally. I was called in on an emergency . . . Oh, no. This isn't making sense." January started pacing.

"That's what I've been trying to explain to you," Carson said.

January shook her head. "I can't believe this is happening. I never did anything to be on anyone's hit list."

"Give her some time," Phoenix said. "She needs to adjust to all this just as much as you did."

January switched her focus, moving closer to the screen where the red beeps still pulsated. "How far away is this?"

"That is about," Phoenix made a ticking noise, "four, five miles away."

"Where's my uniform?" Her next question was directed to Carson.

His mouth parted, and January suspected he was about to lie about it.

"We destroyed it," Phoenix said. "Sorry, kiddo. Can't take any chances."

"What chances?" she asked, close to losing her cool.

"What are you hoping to do, exactly?" Carson asked.

"I'm going after whoever it is. If it's a Ghost, I'll see what his mission is. If he's a jumper . . ." She shrugged.

"Listen, sweetheart—"

"Phoenix, don't. Okay? Just . . . don't. You two may be able to sit back and observe the events unfolding beneath your nose, but I have to do something."

Carson and Phoenix both let out a heavy sigh. Carson said, "Fine, but I'm coming with you."

"That's not—"

"I wasn't asking. You're already wounded. Two Ghosts are better than one, right?"

She narrowed her eyes, catching on to the fact that he planned something that could potentially get her killed.

"I promise to work with you and let you take the lead."

Well, how about that? "Okay, deal, but . . ."

"But?" he asked, lifting a single eyebrow in a smooth motion, making January want to bite her lip. She sighed, letting a smile pull her plump lips. "You know what? You'll figure it out."

He shook his head. "If you say so. Com' on, I'll take you to get geared up."

He turned his back to her and headed for a different door from the room. January let her gaze shift to Phoenix. He smiled and shook his head.

"You two are really something," he muttered as he continued typing away.

***

Geared up meant jeans, a long-sleeved shirt with patches on the shoulders, a heavy vest, and holsters for the legs and waist, complete with pistols.

"This is hardly what I thought you meant by geared up. I thought you made some alterations to the normal uniforms."

Carson shrugged. "It's a lot better than going out there with nothing."

"True, but, why so much heavy stuff? How does someone run with all this extra weight?"

"You'll get used to it."

They moved through the building, pausing at some doors covered in black sheets of construction tarp. Bits of light shone through the thinner parts, making them appear more like a sick reddish-brown. Carson pushed through first, stepping out into a parking garage covered in graffiti and lacking in vehicles. The only one she could see was a large white van without any windows on the sides.

January followed Carson to the exact one. "You have got to be kidding me."

Carson turned around. "What?"

"This?" she shoved a thumb in the direction of the van.

"Yeah. And?"

She shook her head and stepped to the passenger door while muttering under her breath something to the effect of "this is a waste of time," and "thought we were supposed to be *under the radar*," and "ridiculous piece of machinery."

The van shifted. January peeked through the window as Carson reached over and pulled up on the door lock, prompting her to roll her eyes and bite the inside of her cheek. She really missed her own time. Things were easier, simpler, and less complicated. Three things that would normally equate to the same thing, but for January, they were very different.

Carson slid the key into the ignition then gave it a turn. The van growled to life after a few moments.

"That's my girl!"

January stared hard at her *partner*. The idea anyone would so much as equate anything human to such low-tech monstrosities was beyond her.

Carson slipped the gears into reverse, pulled out of the spot they were parked in, and drove in a semi-circle toward the exit with January gripping the door and armrest of her seat.

***

Carson pulled the van close to the curb in front of a thrift store with mannequins standing guard in the windows, wearing mismatched clothing in bright colors and patterns. January wondered how the human race made it past this time with such god-awful style and culture. Still, it could've been worse, she supposed. This could've been the time she called home.

"This should be close to the point of the burst," Carson said, drawing January's attention.

"Fabulous," she muttered. "Now what?"

"You okay?"

She shrugged. "Fine. Why?"

"You seem tense. I need you level headed."

Her eyes shot daggers at him for implying she was anything but. "I'm fine. Let's do this."

He let out a heavy breath before exiting the van. January followed suit, meeting him in front of the monstrous chunk of sheet metal scrap.

Carson glanced at the device on his wrist then pointed toward the park and said, "Right over there. That's where we will find the jumper."

January pursed her brow. "Well, thereabouts."

Carson smiled. January ignored its effect. Instead, she swept a hand in the direction they needed to go, indicating he should take the lead since he was so hell-bent on going. He took the gesture, walking along the sidewalk, weaving between people on bikes, skates, and boards, as well as those who were trying to do their shopping or enjoy a simple cup of coffee in metal chairs and tables with small umbrellas sticking out the middle of them, which couldn't possibly hold much purpose other than to stand there and look pretty.

They made their way to the park, blending in when they needed and checking their surroundings for the other Ghost. It could be anyone. And that made it even more dangerous. January worried about a showdown in the middle of the crowd. There would be no way to cover up that evidence. The event would alter the historical timeline and affect the future in ways that could only be speculated. Despite the worry, January kept her calm. The last thing she or anyone else needed was to lose her "level-headedness" and get someone killed, or worse.

Crossing the street was easy enough with the light on the other end flashing a bright white silhouette walking. Or maybe the image was supposed to depict running, as there wasn't nearly enough time for a normal person to cross before it changed to an orange-red hand.

Following the directions displaying on Carson's wrists (which January made note of asking about later), they made their way to a relatively secluded corner of the park, wooded and shaded from prying eyes. The location didn't surprise January or Carson as that was what most typical Ghosts would choose. What wasn't typical was found as soon as January found her, limping and holding onto her torso, auburn hair falling into her face.

"Michelle," she said in low voice. She took off for her amidst Carson's plea to wait. January ignored him, concerned for her friend who wasn't trained for jumping. She was only a desk worker, a paper pusher who researched the jumps and suspects. Never actual jumping.

Michelle set her hazel eyes on her friend, a flash of relief shown through them, then they darkened. "No! You shouldn't have come."

"What? Why?" January asked as Carson caught up to her.

"It's a trap, Jan." Her eyes rolled into the back of her head as she collapsed to the ground. January rushed to her side and checked for a pulse. Still alive. She breathed a sigh of relief, her gaze raking over the park and the shadows.

Carson did the same, weapon in hand and ready for action. He nodded toward the trees. "Stay here with your friend. I think I see something."

"Wait. No. You need—"

Too late, he was already out of earshot and stepping into the collection of trees and bushes. She turned her gaze back to her friend, worried about her wellbeing and growing dizzy from all the questions running circles through her mind.

"You're not going to believe this," Carson said as he returned.

January lifted her gaze to his, not in the mood to play his guessing games. "What, Carson?"

He cleared his throat, a crease appearing between his eyebrows. "I've never heard of this happening, except in the first few jumps. But, the guy ended up in a tree. We have to get him out of it before anyone else sees him. Besides, he'll start to stink up the area. There'll be no way to keep that from getting back.

True.

That's usually how they checked the success of each Ghost. There would be some report somewhere that headquarters could find. There wasn't a recorded second the Union couldn't get their hands on. They were the rulers, so to speak, of January's time. The gatekeepers.

"We need to get her help, quick, or she'll die." January returned her attention to her friend.

"I'll go get the van. Can you get her to the closest corner?"

January glanced up in time to see he pointed in a specific direction. She nodded. As soon as Carson took off for the death trap, January carefully picked up her friend. Michelle groaned but was able to stand with January's help.

"It's okay, Mickie. We're going to get you some help. Stay with me as long as you can."

She groaned again, then went limp. January responded, pulling her friend up and hiking her over her shoulder. It may not have been the most comfortable or inconspicuous way of getting her friend to the van, but it worked. She could form a reasonable excuse if needed. This time period was noted for its recreational experimentations, so blaming it on booze or something could be easily done. January got her friend to the corner and searched for Carson, but both he and the van were gone without a trace.

Shit.

An annoying sound blared in short spats, growing louder by the second. She turned and faced the direction where it came from and realized Carson was being chased by another Ghost.

This is going to be fun.

Carson hastily pulled up to the curb. January barely got to the back of the van as shots echoed through the air. She flinched when a couple of bullets hit the door. She turned, taking a seat on the floor and tossing her friend behind the other door for protection. Carson forced the van to accelerate hard, nearly causing January to fall out just as a bullet grazed her face. She hollered, bracing herself against the other door and the frame of the van's side. Once she had her balance, she pulled the door closed then carefully arranged her friend into a more comfortable position. Once she was done, she rejoined Carson in the front.

"Now what do we do?" she asked.

He shrugged. "They will either run out of bullets or lose us. This is a big city, so it won't be hard."

January nodded and clung to the door and armrest again, praying the chase would end sooner rather than later. Her friend needed help, and she couldn't wait for it for much longer.

***

Too much time passed. They couldn't shake their pursuers as quickly as January had hoped. Michelle wasn't doing well when she checked in on her, before Carson carried her back into the facility. Even Phoenix said things would be touch and go for a while before they would see any real change in her friend's condition. But that was only if she was going to get better. As it was, Michelle had to be the one to decide to live.

January sat next to her friend's side, holding her hand and sliding her thumb back and forth. She never had the time to process everything before then. She'd been so concerned about getting her friend to safety, that she didn't stop to think about why she was there or how she ended up becoming a part of the trap.

The answers would have to wait for her friend's revival. One thing remained certain: she was now a fugitive in a time she didn't belong to. Going back would mean her death . . . if she went back alone. Yet, the longer she thought about it, the more she realized she was drugged before her jump, and the only person she saw before preparing for the mission was her father. That was the only remaining hazy detail; the time between seeing her father and her jumping, that is. If only there was some way for her to get to her father and ask him what happened.

She would get those answers. She needed them. But for now, she'd wait for her friend to recover and bide her time, blending in as much as possible.

So much for a routine jump, she thought. She shifted her gaze to Carson's. His eyes locked onto hers. *I know you're hiding something too. I'll find out, eventually. I'm a very patient woman, Carson, and secrets have a habit of wanting to be found.*

He nodded once toward her, unknowingly acknowledging January's thoughts. She nodded back, then turned her gaze back to her friend.

Hang in there, Mickie.

***

[Time travel is] neat to think about. I know we've obtained some pretty stellar advances in just my time, and I know that the technology scientists are mastering right now is getting closer and closer to understanding the more complex ideals such as time travel and space travel, so who knows? I think it's possible. Whether that's something that will actually happen or not remains to be seen. Shows like Continuum, Dr. Who, Time Cop, The Time Machine, etc., plus my own fascination with time travel and science fiction [inspired The Ghosts of Time].

Samantha LaFantasie

MEET THE AUTHORS

Samantha LaFantasie - "Ghost of Time"
USA Today Bestselling Fantasy Author

A Kansas native, Samantha LaFantasie spends her free time with her spouse and three kids. Writing has always been a passion of hers, forgoing all other desires to devote to this one obsession, even though she often finds herself arguing with her characters through much of the process. She's primarily a fantasy writer but often feels pulled to genres such as sci-fi, romance, and others.

Samantha became a bestselling author with the Pandora Boxed Set (which includes Made to Forget: Nepherium Novella series--Part One) on major ebook retailers and USA Today. Samantha loves to take time to enjoy other activities such as photography and playing her favorite game of all time, Guild Wars 2.

Visit Samantha's Blog at: http://samanthalafantasie.com

Alesha Escobar - "Logan 6"
Top 100 Historical Fantasy Bestselling Author

Alesha Escobar writes fantasy to support her chocolate habit. She enjoys everything from Tolkien and Dante to the Dresden Files and Hellblazer comics. She resides in California with her partner-in-crime, Luis Escobar, a 20-year art veteran on The Simpsons television show.

Alesha is the author of *The Gray Tower Trilogy*, an action-packed supernatural spy thriller set in an alternate 1940's. The trilogy books have hit the bestsellers lists for Historical Fantasy and Mashups. You can find Alesha at her weekly blog, *Fantasy, Mashups, & Mayhem*, where she discusses fantasy and science fiction TV shows, movies and books, and celebrity gossip. She's just kidding about the celebrity gossip.

Visit Alesha's Blog at http://www.aleshaescobar.com

Timothy C. Ward - "Staring Into"
Science Fiction Author and Hugo Award Nominee

Timothy C. Ward grew up on DragonLance, Stephen King, and Dune. He blends these influences in his serialized epic, *Scavenger*, where sand divers uncover death and evolution within America's buried fortresses. His first printed story, "The Bomb in the President's Bathroom," was released in the Amish SciFi anthology, *Tales from Pennsylvania*. Signed copies are available in his store: Spike Publishing.

Learn more about Tim and his books at
http://www.timothycward.com/my-books/

H.M. Jones - "The Lightstorm of 2015"
B.R.A.G Medallion Fantasy Author

H.M. Jones won the Indie B.R.A.G Medallion for her self-published debut fantasy novel, Monochrome, in 2014. She also writes poetry and is responsible for the *Attempting to Define* poetry collection. A bestseller only in her mind, Jones pays the electric bill by teaching college English courses at night, and is responsible for wrangling her two preschoolers during the day. Thankfully, she is married to a handsome lawyer, since they have other bills to pay. She reads, bookstore hops, writes and moderates and reviews for the indie review site Elite Indie Reads in her "spare" time. Jones received her B.A. and M.A. degrees in English Literature and now lives in the

Pacific Northwest with her family and her very fat cat, Pepper.

Visit H.M.'s blog at https://www.hmjones.net

Devorah Fox - "Turning the Tide"
Top 100 Bestselling Fantasy Author

"What if?" Those two words all too easily send Devorah Fox spinning into flights of fancy. Best-selling author of *The Lost King*, *The King's Ransom*, and *The King's Redress* in The Bewildering Adventures of King Bewilliam literary fantasy series, she also co-authored the contemporary thriller, *Naked Came the Sharks* with Jed Donellie. Devorah published and edited the BUMPERTOBUMPER® books for commercial motor vehicle drivers and developed the Easy CDL test prep apps. Born in Brooklyn, New York, she now lives in The Barefoot Palace in Port Aransas on the Texas Gulf Coast where she writes her "Dee-Scoveries" blog.

Visit Devorah's Blog at http://devorahfox.com

Alice Marks - "End of the Road"
Author and Educator

Retired early childhood educator, Alice has been married for 50 years and has four adult children and six grandchildren. She is a resident of Duluth, Minnesota, the second coldest city in the USA, which affords lots of time for writing. Alice has published short stories and poetry in magazines and anthologies, including Chicken Soup for the Soul. She wrote the life story of a 105-year-old Texas woman, whose family published the memoir. She has written several comedic Biblical plays, which have been used by Readers' Theatres in several states and has led a writers group In Texas, is currently forming one in Duluth, and teaches creative writing classes for emerging writers. She has a drawer full of novels waiting publication.

STORY EXCERPTS

Find More Amazing Sci-Fi & Fantasy Reads!

Thank you for purchasing (or gifting) this copy of MASTERS OF TIME. If you enjoyed these stories, please show your support by sharing your review online at Amazon, Barnes and Noble, or another online retailer. Your opinion matters!

In this special paperback edition, we're also including excerpts from some of our authors' other popular works. If their imagination and creativity spoke to you through Masters of Time, imagine what their full-length novels will do for you. Turn the page and enjoy!

THE KING'S REDRESS

By Devorah Fox

The novel-in-progress that held claim to the front burner when I first drafted *Turning the Tide* was *The King's Redress*, Book Three of *The Bewildering Adventures of King Bewilliam*, an epic fantasy series. At this point in the saga, Robin—King Bewilliam—finds that there is no one he can trust, not even his closest knights. In this scene, Robin takes on one of his own knights in a surprising final "mano a mano" that caps a grueling three-day jousting tournament.

***

"Henry has won." Prince Zachary fairly gloated. "He is the ultimate victor."

"Not so fast," said Robin. "There is one more challenger."

"There is? But no shields remain on the tree," Zachary said.

Even as he said it, Robin knew it could be a mistake. He called to the seneschal, "We accept the challenge."

The seneschal gaped, eyebrows raised. "But Your Majesty …."

It wasn't unheard of for a king to participate in a tournament but it was unwise, even risky. He could be injured or killed, but the potential danger was burned to a cinder by Robin's red-hot rage. "Announce it."

The seneschal bowed and passed the word to the herald who declared that there would be yet another contestant, King Bewilliam himself.

Behind him, Sir Maxwell said, "Begging your pardon, Your Majesty, but is that wise?"

Zachary cried, "Sire, you can't, you shouldn't," but the protests were a meaningless murmur lost in the roaring in Robin's ears and the stomp of his boots as he descended the grandstand's steps.

Maxwell trotted up behind him.

"Sir Maxwell, get our armor." Safely stored in the armory there was little likelihood that anyone had interfered with it. "Let's see what Sir Henry can do against a fighter who hasn't been sabotaged by faulty equipment. Get our horse."

"Hope, Sire? But Hope is no destrier."

"No, but he's a good sturdy courser. He's fast and strong and agile and we have become a good team. He will respond to our instructions and we do know what instructions to give. And we want those spurs that we designed." The king's spurs were not simply a pick affixed to a heel band but a more versatile rowel, a star-shaped wheel with sharpened points that rotated on a shaft. "And get us an ale."

Robin's nerves twanged, his blood sang, and his muscles twitched in anticipation. He felt light on his feet like the youth he had been the last time he jousted. That may have been some years ago but he hadn't forgotten the moves nor lost his edge.

Sir Henry signaled for the seneschal and their heads leaned together. The seneschal nodded, approached Robin, and bowed.

"Sire, Sir Henry is honored to have such an esteemed opponent. He wishes you to know that he promises to grant no favors nor hobble himself due to his opponent's status."

Robin didn't miss the insinuation. He knew that Sir Henry's statement wasn't a promise. *Was it a question: did Robin expect special treatment? Or was it a dare?* "Indeed, we would expect no less than Sir Henry's best effort," Robin replied, trying not to sound sarcastic. "We would be offended by anything less. We intend to fight fairly according to the rules."

While they waited for Sir Maxwell to return with Robin's armor, Sir Henry paced.

Let him carve a path in front of his pavilion and burn off what is left of his drive. Robin thought Sir Henry would be wiser to rest but he was pleased at Henry's agitation, a sign perhaps of apprehension.

Pacing wasn't a bad idea though. Walking would help Robin to warm and stretch muscles stiffened by a day of sitting. As well, Sir Henry might think that his adversary was nervous. It might give Sir Henry false confidence.

You are mine. Robin breathed deeply and set his jaw. He realized with a start that he no longer thought of Sir Henry as his own vassal whose loyalty was an important element of the Chalklands' security. Instead, the man was a foe to be vanquished.

DARK RIFT

By Alesha Escobar

Dark Rift is the Amazon bestselling second book of the Gray Tower Trilogy (and you can pick up the first book, *The Tower's Alchemist*, in ebook format for free!). Some have said it's like Agent Carter, but with a supernatural twist. Since I'm a big fan of Marvel's Agent Carter show, this is a huge compliment. Please enjoy this excerpt, and don't forget to download your free copy of the first book of this trilogy today.

***

I carved the alchemical symbol for Fire in the waiting room's doorframe--a triangle. My head swam from the protective seal Nena had placed on my mind, but I managed to swat her hand away when she reached for the doorknob. I raised my trembling index finger to my lips in a gesture for her to remain quiet, and I charged my Fire symbol with magical energy, feeding it with mental concentration.

I unlocked the door and swung it open. The Cruenti warlock was gone. He may have worn an expensive black suit and appeared innocuous with his slight frame, but my senses had gone off and screamed for me to run. I breathed a low sigh and decided to obey my instincts. I had rushed into the waiting room, my eyes on the exit just across from me, when something wet splashed onto my forehead. I immediately looked up to see the warlock plastered to the ceiling, salivating and watching me with his electric blue eyes. I swung my knife just in time to slice his chest as he landed on me. I fell into a roll with him and ended up on top. As I drove the blade toward his heart, he sent me flying backward with an invisible force. I crashed against a few folding chairs lined up against the wall and dropped my golden knife. I cursed at Nena in my head for having invited the warlock in.

My head still throbbed from the mind seal, and I hardly had time to react when he rushed me and bared his elongated canines. I threw my arms up in a defensive position when he reached me, and he bit into my right forearm. I growled in pain.

"Morgan, don't eat her!" Nena shrieked.

I swung a left hook and nailed him right in the face. When he locked onto my arm like a pit bull, I howled and threw all my weight into a pivot, and we both hit the floor. He drew back when Nena screamed and smashed his head with a potted plant. He snarled at her, and she fell back. I rolled over toward my knife on the floor, grabbing it just as Morgan caught me by the ankle and twisted the bone. I heard a crack and screamed at the searing pain that shot through my leg. I used my good foot to kick at his face, which now resembled a rabid animal's.

The Cruenti crawled onto me and went for my neck. I held him at bay with my injured arm, and his swollen tongue, full of purple splotches, darted toward my face. I gripped my knife and made a few deep cuts into his torso. He shrieked and backed off to allow the wounds to regenerate. I jumped to my feet and nearly collapsed on my broken ankle. I eyed the doorframe where I had laid my Fire symbol and limped toward it. Nena stood in the little adjacent room, gripping another folding chair and using it as a shield once I made it inside. When he glided toward us, I released the Fire symbol, and his head lit up like a torch.

The putrid smell of burnt flesh filled the room, he ran and jumped out of the waiting room's window. I cast a Circle of Protection around the little house and leaned against the doorframe for support. I still felt light-headed from Nena's mind seal, and tears stung my eyes from the pain in my arm and broken ankle.

"I'm sorry, Isabella," Nena cried. "He's been my client for four weeks and has never done that before."

"Are you sure?" I motioned toward my purse with a weak hand.

"Grab my satchel with the jade powder."

The gypsy woman did as instructed--and took a few crisp bills while she was at it. "He told me he's been a Cruenti for five years, but wanted treatment. He said that he was starting to change into a Black Wolf, and if Octavian can be a powerful Cruenti without being transformed into a Wolf, then why can't he."

"Well, he should've worried about the side effects *before* becoming a Cruenti." I opened my satchel and sprinkled the jade powder on my arm. I lowered myself to the floor and rubbed it into my ankle. The jade stone had healing properties, and I would purchase it in small quantities from time to time. It was expensive as hell, but well worth it in my line of work.

"He paid me good money to help treat him," Nena said, adjusting her ugly plaid dress. "He said he wasn't eating wizards anymore."

Cruenti warlocks made pacts with demons to obtain special powers, and they satisfied the bond through Blood Magic, where they'd feed on other wizards and drain them of their powers. The worst part was that in order to be initiated, you had to use an innocent person as a sacrifice. Some normal people were crazy enough to become initiates, or sycophants, because they wanted to gain magical abilities, even though they weren't born with any.

I closed my satchel and waited for the agony in my limbs to subside. "Nena, you can't treat or cure a Cruenti. I'm surprised he hasn't ripped your throat out and stolen your powers."

"I swear to you, I wouldn't have let Morgan in if I knew he would react that way to you." Nena half-heartedly offered me ten dollars from the stack of bills she had swiped.

We both jumped when the Cruenti banged on the window of the little room we were in. He called out to Nena. "I didn't mean to scare you. It's your friend. She's...different."

"Go away." Nena ran and shut her curtain.

"Send her out to me, Nena." We heard a crash against the wall, but he couldn't break my Circle of Protection.

Nena scrambled to her closet and pulled out a staff. It stood four feet tall--the same height as Nena--and looked like a gnarled wooden arm. She slid her hands palm down and gripped the staff as she raised it and struck the floor. "Leave my property, or I will lay a curse on you such as you have never seen."

He crashed against the wall once more and let out a strangled cry.

Nena pounded her staff again and what looked like lightening shot across the floor. It moved toward the window where he stood. This time, I felt his magic, and his presence, pull away and leave.

I drew in a deep breath, and my heart thumped painfully in my chest. I rose to my feet and went for my purse, all the while glaring at Nena. Not only did she almost get me killed, but she was also going to make me miss my ride. Word had come that the Nazis were sending in tanks to Odessa today, and if I didn't meet my contact, who could give me a ride out of the territory, then I'd have to scramble down to the port and ride across the Black Sea.

"I feel bad about Morgan." She mumbled something under her breath and took out a cigarette. She snapped her fingers and produced a flame. "Let me make it up to you."

"Are you going to give me back the last half hour of my life?"

"Well, in case you're interested, Delana made it to Baltimore. She has Agate stone."

Hmm, I probably would pay the other woman a visit. I would be on my way to the United States next week to be with my family. "Bye, Nena. And don't let Morgan come back. He'll probably try to eat you."

"So...what is it?" she asked.

"What do you mean?"

"What is it that makes you different?"

I shrugged my shoulders. "Maybe it's because I'm a *Tower Slave*." I had always hated that epithet. People hurled it as an insult toward wizards trained by the Gray Tower.

SCAVENGER

By Timothy C. Ward

In a world buried to the nose in sand, Rush felt no choice but to let his ears live for him. River's moan slipped through the floorboards above him like a last desperate cry not to give up. There was life left to scavenge.

The soft and gentle releasing of breath drifted and disappeared into the belly of the Honey Hole, a tavern that reeked of stale beer and dried sweat.

Rush brushed his fingernail through sand embedded in the cracks of his table. His dream had once been discovering the buried city, Danvar, where the wood was unmarked and smooth, where he'd bring up enough spoil to make all of Springston live like lords.

That dream died with his son.

River's elongated cry soured in his heart's infection, where the memory of seeing his son face down in sand had cut open his soul and left him to the death that never ended.

Set near his hand was the mug of ale River's appointment had left. He had dropped it off with a cocky grin and, "I'll make her nice and loud for ya."

Now he lay on a naked and sweating River.

Rush took a drink.

A man stood from a table across the tavern, leaving his compatriot head-over-folded-arms drunk. He looked at Rush, glanced down at the drunk, and pushed in his chair. The ker draped around his neck was bright orange with a horse's head emblazoned in white fire. Even the tower dwellers on the East side couldn't afford such vibrant colors. The pale cheeks and pink-red tan line cutting from nose to ear and circling his eyes identified him as someone unaccustomed to the hardness of a sun-burnt lifestyle. His gaze locked on Rush with pride in his distinction.

The man took a chair from a neighboring table and had a seat close enough to be brother or threat. He leaned in and whispered, "I hear you're Rushing, Springston's famous divemaster."

The honor of his past once again refused to leave him. Rush took another drink.

"I also hear you haven't parted the sand in years."

Rush glowered over the rim of his mug.

"I don't mean to cause waves, but I've got a job offer that could use your talents."

He hadn't had a decent job since Fisher died. Still. "I don't dive."

"Right. You shuffle a mop around a filthy whorehouse and drink warm beer while your favorite girl gets rowdy." The man split a grin worth cutting off. "That's a much better alternative."

Rush set his mug down carefully. "Would you like to see what else I can do with a mop?"

"Hey, I like that. And here I was, afraid you'd lost the vigor that made you the best."

River's panting increased in intensity. He nodded up at the balcony. "I hear you've never had the pleasure."

"I think it's time you parted sand, stranger. Whatever you're offering, I'm not interested."

Stranger leaned closer. His artificial scent matched the man's who'd given him his beer. Rush smelled a setup.

"Is money the reason you haven't...?" he double clicked his tongue and mimicked an ornery cat.

Why hadn't Rush met this guy the day he quit the school? He could have opened up a hole thirty feet deep and left diving in fashion.

Stranger went on as if his company was still welcome, "I've seen your tent, Rush. Not exactly the home you used to have, from what I hear. Is it?"

"You sure hear a lot that ain't your business."

"I hear only what is my business."

What does that mean? "Okay…what's your name?"

"Warren."

"Okay, Warren. The reason I haven't is I'm still married."

"You wouldn't be the first married bloke to slip between a whore's legs."

As if on cue, River let out her climaxed cry. Rush thought of the pleasure he had known making Star gasp the same way. It had been years.

"Besides, I hear you two are about as much in love as the sweaty cheeks I'm sitting on."

"You hear…whatever business you have in Springston, I suggest you take it elsewhere."

"I'm afraid that's not possible."

Rush wanted to say, "You better make it possible," but something told him he needed to find out why. "Lay your cards, Warren."

"All right!" Warren slapped imaginary cards on the table, burping a bit of beer from Rush's mug. One of the bar members glanced over his shoulder, but returned to his drink without alarm.

Warren inched close, revealing a gold tooth in his back row. "I have a very important job that could use someone of your skills, but I wasn't about to offer it without a little digging into your present state."

A very important job could be just what he needed. Something to distract him.

Warren seemed to read Rush's thoughts. "I'm ready to pay you enough for one dive—" he lifted a finger toward the balcony "—to do…whatever you want, for as long as you want it."

Whatever job a stranger offered for that kind of price shouldn't be worth the filth it would leave behind.

Unless you were Rush, and were already buried in it. He didn't have to use that money on River. Maybe just leaving would be enough. He took another swig of the free drink and let the warmth numb his fears. "Working here has diminished the value of talk."

Warren dropped a purple coin purse heavy enough to buy a trip as far away as he needed, even if it only had coppers. If it had gold…

He noticed Rush's interest, his hitched breath, and smiled. "And that's just a down payment."

Just like that, he could be free of this Hell. But his attachment to Star, a marriage as unwanted as the dirt under his nails, tugged at his conscience. River came back to mind, like a knife ready to use. Lying with her could break him free for good. And he'd be alive again, if only for a moment. As estranged as he was from Star, he didn't know why he felt guilt. They were worse than strangers.

But too weak to say goodbye.

He didn't care what the job was. *I won't let you keep me here anymore.* "I'll do it."

"All right, Rush is back." Warren slapped his arm.

Rush squeezed the coins inside the purse. Metal that couldn't satisfy his true needs, but metal nonetheless. To a poor man, it was something.

"Now, first order of business." Warren helped Rush up by the arm and guided him to the drunk passed out on his table. A hint of copper tainted the air. He forced Rush to stand beside the man while he stood, back to the bar, and looked at the floor.

Rush followed his gaze to a pool of blood seeping through cracks in the wood. The man was as still as Rush had feared.

Warren whispered, "I can kill you just as easy."

None of the bar patrons gave a lick about his sudden danger. "Why would you kill me?"

"If you don't follow through with your end."

In spite of the new weight squeezing his ribs, he shouldn't have expected his exit from Springston to be easy. Rush did not back down.

"Good, now follow me." Warren slid a knife back into a sleeve at his belt.

The sleeve was somehow familiar. *You didn't even see him reach for it.*

Rush wanted one of the three bar patrons to glance over their shoulders as he left, ask him where he was going, who the stranger was and who the corpse was they had left behind, but none noticed. Rush was the guy that cleaned up their semen and vomit. They hadn't noticed him in years.

MADE TO FORGET

By Samantha LaFantasie

Not long after the doctor left, I turned my attention to Jenna. "You've gotta give me some answers."

"I can try to answer your questions, but I don't know much more than you right now." She gazed out the window as if she was less than interested in playing along.

"What do you know about this accident?" I asked, carefully watching her reaction.

She sighed, almost impatiently, but also sadly. "I know that it was a full transporter at takeoff, but you were the only one found."

"I was the only one that survived?"

"No," she said sharply, turning her gaze to me. "I said you were the only one found."

"I don't understand."

"Neither do I," said a man's voice. Deep and luring. My guard popped up instantly, and a chill trickled along my spine.

I turned my attention to a tall brunette with dark eyes and a smile that looked more like he wanted me for dinner than he was glad to see me. Completely feral. He wore a long, standard military trench coat with black slacks and shiny, black shoes. He kept his hands in his coat pockets and leaned against the corner of the wall as if he materialized there. I definitely hadn't heard the door open.

"Who are you?" I asked, attempting to keep my voice even.

"Do you not recognize me?" He smiled again. I swore I could see the venom. The dimple on one side of his face bothered me, like

104

there should have been one on the other side. But even that wasn't quite it. There was history. A dark history. My palms itched and my heart fluttered faster. I wanted to run or fight. Not engage in more banter.

"That seems to be the popular question for today. 'No—I don't—should I?' is usually the question I ask in return."

He chuckled quietly. "Yes, you should, but given the circumstances, I understand why you don't."

I nodded slowly. "Uh huh …"

"I'm Alexander Barabbas," he said, then shifted his gaze to Jenna. "Could you excuse us for a few moments?"

Immediately, she stood and walked out of the room, keeping her focus on the floor as she passed him. I raised an eyebrow at her, then shifted my gaze back to him. He watched Jenna walk out, turning his head as she passed, then slowly returned his attention to me.

MONOCHROME

By H.M. Jones

"Another young one." A careful tenor voice murmured above her head. Abigail forced her eyes open, but her vision was still fuzzy.

"Waking up, are you?" The voice belonged to a dark blur hovering over her body. "It's fine. The trip here does this to everyone. Take your time," the blur advised her.

She was able to rub her eyes with heavy, still tingling hands. She blinked her leaden lids and her eyes gradually focused. The dark blur became a man wearing a black wool hat and a charcoal pea-coat with a large, impressive collar.

Panic bubbled like acid in her stomach. *How did this man get into my house? Is my baby okay? Why can't I hear her?* With a start, Abigail tried to shoot up from the ground, only to bang her head against a hard, jagged object behind her.

"Ow! What the...," she started.

"Slow down. It's a rough trip, lady."

Abigail grasped around for something to defend herself with. Her fingernails scrapped across what felt like Easter basket grass made of aluminum foil. Confusion overcame her fear. She held her hands up. They were covered in a shimmering, powdery dust. She was not in her room, not at home, not in the city, in fact. All around her were tall, navy colored trees, and silver-blue grass. Somewhere in the distance she heard the flow of a body of water.

The nature around her was covered in a blue-tinted twilight. *He must have taken me to the woods. But where? I didn't think there were woods anywhere near where we lived.* Everything could not be blue. It was the mixture of her blurred vision and shock of waking to nature at night. *It must be.* She searched for the glowing moon in the sullen cerulean sky, but was unable to spot it. A mysterious silver light settled on the midnight scene, coming from nowhere and everywhere.

"Where am I? Why have you taken me here? Where's my baby!" Abigail shot questions at the dark stranger, who calmly took a seat on the trunk of a tall, thin, fallen tree.

The stranger fiddled around in his jacket pocket and pulled out a pack of cigarettes and a lighter. "Look, I'll explain to you the situation as best as I can, but you have to promise not to freak out on me. I hate when they freak out. I mean, it's part of the job, but it gets tiring."

He paused, watched her from under his wool hat, put a cigarette in his mouth and lit it. Abigail was stunned into silence. *What the hell is this guy talking about? He brought me here on a job? What kind of job?* She shuddered to think of what this meant for her.

She stood and backed slowly away from the stranger, who noticed but made no move to stop her, except to say, "Please don't run. I'm here to help and it would be very counterproductive since there is nowhere you can run where I can't find you."

He inhaled deeply from his cigarette and looked askance at her. "Shit, sorry, lady. I guess that sounded like a threat." Smoke billowed out from between his lips as he spoke. "It wasn't."

He blew the remainder of the drag through his lips. "You smoke?" He lifted the pack of cigarettes towards Abigail in offering. She ignored the gesture, took a deep breath and another step back. She was still shocked at the turn of events and worried about her baby, but first she needed to find out where she was, so she could get home.

She gathered her courage. "I won't turn my back on you to run. Plus," she added, hoping her voice sounded firm even with fear racing through her veins, "I'm not afraid of you. If you come near me, I will kill you." She was proud of herself. Her voice was icy and composed. She even managed to keep her hands from shaking by making fists.

The dark stranger removed his wool hat, ran his hand through shoulder-length, dark blonde hair and grunted in amusement. "So...you don't smoke? Hope you don't mind if I do because I will regardless." He took another drag of his cigarette and tilted his head towards her. "You can sit. I promise to give you no reason to kill me, and from the sound of your voice, you are confident you could."

He shook his head and offered a tired smile. "I don't want to rush you, but perhaps you want to know where you are and why you're here?"

Abigail relaxed her fists. She didn't know the man in front of her but she understood without knowing him he meant her no harm. His was the air of someone who went out of his way to do as little as possible. She moved closer to the stranger. "I want to know my baby is okay. The rest can wait."

She leaned towards the dark stranger, hopeful.

"Your baby?" The man's eyebrows drew down in confusion.

"Yes. My *baby*, asshole! The baby screaming in my house when you took me away." She her stomach twist into knots, again.

"Okay." The stranger held his hands up in front of him, one still holding a lit cigarette. "First, *I* didn't bring you here. *You* did." Abigail made to interrupt him but he continued. "Second, your baby is *where* you left it. In the same *state* you left it. In the same *time* you left it."

Abigail raised a baffled eyebrow at the man in front of her. He didn't give her the chance to ask another question. He calmly put his hat back on his head. "I mean, your baby is fine as long as it was fine when you left it. Time moves more slowly here."

He took a drag from his cigarette and sat back in a relaxed position, as if he just answered everything. She could not remember a time when she was more confounded, but her anger subsided. She couldn't be too angry with an insane person. "Okay. Fine. I just want to know how to get back home to my baby, so if you have a car or directions or something..."

She hoped to reason with the lunatic who, for some reason, abducted her. "You're obviously not interested in hurting me. I don't know why you brought me here or what..."

The stranger exhaled, interrupting her. "Look, you're not listening. You aren't the first person I've led to think I am crazy," he said, reading her tone correctly. "And you won't be the last."

He took a final drag of his cigarette, flicked it away and crushed the butt under a black, buckled boot. "Again, I didn't take you here and 'here' is not the place you were before. This place is called Monochrome and you are here because you didn't want to be where you were."

Her tolerance quoted was filled. This man's crazy talk was holding her up. She stalked toward him, grabbed his coat collar between clenched fists and shook him.

"Listen, asshole, tell me how to get home or, so help me God, I'll make you wish you'd never met me." She didn't raise her voice. She knew the rage distorting her face was proof enough to convince him to stop playing with her.

The stranger tilted his hat up and peered into her light green eyes with eyes the color of tar. *No, not tar. Tar does not glimmer.* Abigail thought this man must have swallowed a universe full of stars, so that it would sparkle, deadly, in his eyes. His gaze unnerved her and made her dizzy. She dropped her hands from his collar, her arms shaking and her knees weak.

"Thank you," he stated, unmoved, as he returned to his seat on the fallen tree. Abigail stumbled as she backed away, tripping over the same cold, hard rock she hit her head on upon first waking. She fell backwards and landed on her side.

"I hope you're okay?" The man asked, without a hint of sympathy.

"Fine. Just a scrape on my hand and maybe a bruise on the side of my leg. But don't get up..." She sarcastically shot at the stranger, who went back to his relaxed position on the fallen tree and was now carelessly lighting another cigarette. His face was lit behind the flash of the match, a sulfur tang stinging the air. *He's handsome, for an asshole.*

She sat up from her fall and examined the damage, only to stop short. She remembered putting on a pair of jeans and a flannel this morning. She brushed dust from her side and gasped. Instead of the coarse tightness of denim, her hands slid effortlessly across a length of fabric, cashmere soft.

She stood up and patted her person, looking down in shock at the indigo velvet dress that fell from her hips. The dress bustled in the back. Black buttons dotted her from torso to neck, and black lace cuffs accented the paleness of her skin. The dress was more appropriate for a Victorian romance novel than the twenty-first century.

"Um, what *am* I wearing and where are my old clothes?" Abigail started. "Did you..." she flushed, "change me?"

The man guffawed, offended. "Do I really look that creepy?"

"Well, I didn't change myself and you're the only one I see," she answered. "And, yes, you are a bit creepy, so..."

The stranger's pursed his lips, amused. "You're funny. No, I didn't change you."

He played with his cigarette to avoid her glare. "What you wear *can* reflect what you feel on the inside in this place, though most people here are cognizant enough to go through changes very often. You must feel..."

He scrutinized her dress with midnight eyes. Abigail got the impression if he examined her closely with those eyes, he could see every dark secret she bore. She shivered. "Caged. You feel caged. Lonely. Like I said, most people's wardrobe doesn't really change much, except for color. And it usually derives from something they owned or wore in their other life. But that dress says repressed."

She wore a dress like this to a tea party her friend put on. It was a rental. She almost forgot about that day.

Surprising herself, she retorted, "And you feel bored and apathetic."

She was referring to his black and grey tones, the careless, worn wool hat over slightly disheveled, mussed hair, the charcoal pea-coat over torn jeans. Every piece of fabric, every leisurely gesture, gave the impression he tried very hard to look like he didn't care about how others saw him.

He raised a quizzical eye. "Not exactly. So, are you ready to hear about this place or not, lady?"

"Abigail. Abigail Benet," she insisted.

The man exhaled smoke from his cigarette and nodded in greeting. "Ishmael Dubois."

She shook her head in astonishment. "Perfect. Shall I call you Ishmael, then?"

Ishmael rolled his eyes playfully. "Yes. Call me Ishmael, and I've heard that before. Do you want to know why you're here, Abby?"

She bristled. "Abigail. And I want to know why I am here and when I can go home to my baby and my husband."

Ishmael took another cigarette from his pack and winked at her. "That's the kind of attitude that'll get you out of here fast, Abby."

Abigail moved to sit down on the other end of the fallen tree. She was still dizzy from her fainting spell. Her legs felt like cooked noodles. She placed her hands on the trunk and shivered at its cold, metallic texture. *How strange.* She shook her head to focus and laid her hands on her lap.

"Don't call me Abby. Only friends call me Abby."

Ishmael turned his head to blow smoke away from her and shrugged. "I hope we can be friends."

ABOUT CREATIVE ALCHEMY

Creative Alchemy, Inc. is a small indie publishing company that is passionate about crafting great stories, producing stunning art, and helping artists and writers achieve their goals. Team Creative Alchemy is headed by professional writers, artists, and editors who love science fiction and fantasy.

http://www.thecreativealchemy.com

Made in the USA
Charleston, SC
01 August 2016